For Yiayia

PROLOGUE

"The only thing necessary for the triumph of evil is for good men to do nothing."—Edmund Burke

"*E*leanora!"

It was her. He'd never been so sure. His superior vision, like looking through binoculars, zeroed in on the form that had tormented him for centuries.

Though his eyes were focused across the devastation, tunneled by his ability to see three times as far as any human, his impeccable hearing forced his gaze from her.

Someone's hand emerged from the rubble. Steel, wires and charred drywall surrounded the protruding flesh. It waved in circles, a symbol of hope among chaos. It was a woman's hand. Her nails had been painted pale pink, the tint peeking out behind streams of blood and burns. Elpis couldn't determine the source of the blood, with this many bodies; it may not have been hers. But as he grabbed her hand and squeezed reassurance, he noted the warmth beneath her skin and a thread, but present pulse. As he held this woman's hand, he couldn't resist looking back to catch another glimpse of Eleanora, only feet away.

Averting his gaze back to his task, he looked right then

left. Elpis couldn't help but be overwhelmed by the devastation that surrounded him. He forced his heart to divide between the ache for those he could not save and the need to attend to those he might. Children lay in final sleep, businessmen and women frozen in their last hectic movements of the start of their work day. Survivors sat stunned, or circled aimlessly, blood pouring from where ear drums had been split by the explosion. But it was the smell that lingered, creating a blanket of discomfort from which he could not escape.

In the centuries that Elpis had been fighting, one constant was the odor of burning flesh. Like the sudden presence of fermenting meat, it was acrid. Intensifying the scent, his abilities enabled him to delineate divergent aromas. The hair, for instance, presents itself as sulfuric, like the smell of rotten eggs, while the skin itself, burdened by blood vessels, releases a coppery essence. It is a scent that is relentless and not easily forgotten.

On that day, he had been called in only after the devastation. The concealed bomb had torn through the structure like the arm of God. A young man, perhaps working his first job, coughed incessantly, blood spattering the concrete beneath him. A rescuer pried him from the ground and carried him to a nearby ambulance.

No one would notice if Elpis reacted. *My presence won't be observed in this chaos, and I don't have time to dig her out piece by piece*, he thought to himself.

Pulling the woman slowly but effortlessly from the pile that weighed upon her, he revealed to any onlooker his true strength. But it didn't matter. Elpis cradled her limp body to his chest and forced himself to jog at human speed to the nearest paramedic. Sure that she was in good hands, he turned back to his original purpose.

"Eleanora!"

He called after her, an escalation in his voice that felt foreign even as it exited his lips. With speed he rarely utilized, he forced his position beside her, overtly aware of

2

the heat from her wrist pulsing with the knowledge of his presence. Gently but firmly wrapping his fingers around hers, Elpis forced a calming breath. It took all his focus to evoke the sensation of flesh to flesh; he hadn't done this in some time. He was torn between the elation at the reality that he actually stood beside her, his Eleanora, and horror at the fact that she could have stopped this carnage and chose not to.

She turned. Her precise and painful movement was like peeling the bandages from an injury he believed to be healed. Not hesitant in any way, but with a fierce edge of defiance that caused a shock of pain in him.

After two thousand years, her presence struck him with the ferocity of their history.

Her golden hair cascaded around her, the wind lightly lifting it in a dance around her frame. The soft arch of her skin was a perfection that was just as he remembered. It was a beauty that remained subtle and untried. But her expression had changed. The remnants of dimples were a memory, the softness of her mouth pulled tight, unwavering.

"Elpis..." she spoke his name simply; a pupil on her roster. But the weight behind the name poured out of her. The wind blew around them, sidestepping emotions that pulsed between the two.

Elpis chose anger. "How could you?"

"How could I what?" she spoke with irritation.

He let her go, although he could have held on. "How could you be a part of this? It was you who let this happen." He spoke as much to himself as to the woman before him.

"Why do you defend them? Aren't you weary of all the missions?" Her questions bit at him.

"Over one hundred casualties so far," he said softly.

"I'm aware," she replied coldly. A smile spread across her lips. It didn't reach her eyes, but it unhinged Elpis, nonetheless.

"At least six hundred have been injured! They never saw it coming. Eleanora, there was a daycare in that building. Were those children the evil humanity you were intending to target?"

She took a small step backwards. "Elpis, you know there are casualties of war. You know that better than most. You yourself have turned your back on many." Her words buried nails in his heart, and her shark eyes refused to release him from their prison. "You know how this works. Don't pretend this can't happen. It will happen. It does happen. It *must* happen." Her final words were said in a whisper.

"Why here?" Elpis couldn't help but demand answers he knew he would not get. Not from her. He continued, "Nerve gas in a Tokyo subway...the Israeli Prime Minister... Were you there when he was assassinated? Rawanda..." His voice faded as he saw her weak smile return. Her eyes drew ice to his veins. "The Poneros have been involved in all of that just this year."

She met his gaze, lifting her eyebrows and releasing a breath. "Yes, of course; it was all too easy for *us*." Her words were simply checks in boxes. The wind shifted at that moment, blowing her memories toward Elpis.

He took the moment to inhale her, but smelled only the blood and smoke that she had caused. He closed his eyes, almost in defeat. But before he could let her go, he spoke, "You've tipped the scales, Eleanora."

"If you think so," she retorted.

As she turned, he pulled her chin toward him, and she felt his aged fingers rub the soft skin beneath her mouth. He spoke before she could pull away: "And *we* will tip them back."

CHAPTER ONE

*A*s if looking through cloudy glass, Clara Eros attempted to focus on something familiar, but nothing was recognizable. In fact, her memory was as blank as her vision. Where her identity belonged, there was nothing. And yet she felt no panic; only an odd sense of acceptance. Something had brought her here, and it was here that she belonged.

"Clara? *Tikanis?*"

Startled by the sudden presence of another person in such a private moment, she silently accepted that the speaker was addressing her—she must be 'Clara'. The man standing before her was speaking Greek, a language she was sure she did not understand. Or did she? A familiarity in the man's eyes reminded her of home, but she had no recognition of where that home might exist. She waited with detached conviction, not knowing how to answer his question about her well-being.

"*Protos*," the 'P' and the 'R' rolled eloquently in the Greek elocution of the word 'first.' "The English use the Greek root in their word 'prototype.' And you, Clara, are extremely unique—a prototype in your own way." His fingers softly ran across his thick black mustache, almost in a movement of discovery rather than thought. His matching dark curls matted the top of his head in thick ringlets around his crown, mimicking the swirl of his speech. As his fingers moved, the image of his face fragmented for a moment and then it was gone.

Clara wasn't giving his etymology lesson much thought. She was still rolling her name around in her mouth like melting ice cubes.

"Clara, do I look familiar to you?"

He knew that he was presenting himself, for the moment, in the image of her father, an image that would no doubt illicit feelings of safety and comfort. He also knew she wouldn't quite recognize him. For her, it would seem like waking from a dream she knew to be fantastic, an image remained heartlessly just out of her grasp.

She was now taking notice of her form, as if for the first time. She held her hands before her, letting the light filter between her fingers. It was all so perplexing, but she admired her own curious existence. She turned her hands from side to side noting the olive undertone running from the skin that expanded and disappeared under her soft, white sleeves. Her nails were blunt and smooth, small crevices winked and disappeared as she flexed and stretched her fingers. The lines on the insides of her palms extended in meaningless patterns.

"Let me start at your beginning..."

Clara tried desperately to narrow her sights on something real, yet her very existence seemed unfathomable.

"Today, we begin your preparation." His voice was smooth, his speech delivered with a slight Greek accent. Despite Clara's confusion, his confident manner elicited safety.

"Preparation for what?" Her first words in this new, but not novel, voice came out crisp and clear.

"There's so much... Where do I begin?"

"I don't understand...anything," she said. She felt helpless.

"We are at war," he said.

"You and I?" Clara spit out. Her right eyebrow arched in a way that suggested both amusement and irritation.

He laughed; he couldn't help himself. Laughing did not come easily to him. In fact, these days, laughing was something almost entirely foreign to him. He had forgotten how freeing it felt. He had forgotten much. "No, not you and I."

"Who then?"

Clara struggled for understanding, bouncing thoughts against him as quickly as he made statements. She needed to understand. Understand something, anything.

"For now, let's just say there is a right and there is a wrong. And the two forces are at odds." His face remained stoic, emotionless. His fingers were gently clasped in front of his gray coat. He seemed to know what she would ask before she asked it.

"Does a person ever really know that they are on the *wrong* side?"

"Let me explain what is happening to you." With the tilt of an eyebrow, he acknowledged the gravity of this moment. "What you are experiencing might be considered a kind of birth—or perhaps *rebirth* might be a better term. For now, you are in a period of gestation, for lack of a better metaphor, and once you are prepared for the battle ahead, you will be wholly reborn with the knowledge you have gained. Your body, your life, your very existence on the other side has been compromised for purposes that have been out of your control...until this moment. And for that, I am truly sorry. The only way to enhance the effectiveness of the brain is to tear it down; rewire it for more complex principles. It's an arduous process, and I am not quite sure how to explain this. You are the first.

"On the other side, you lived your life. A full and giving life, but the last years have shown a steep decline in your

7

mental capacity. Physically, your brain has been shrinking, dramatically. Nerve cell death and tissue loss started years ago. However, the cataloguing of what I tell you from today forward will be stored amongst the now empty shelves of your mind. Here you stand, an almost empty vessel, prepared for recalibration of the mind."

He waited, feeling a little smug about the concise nature of his explanation. His eyes still watched her closely. So swiftly, it may not have happened, he thought he saw her strain. And then it was gone. Was that pain? He cringed at the thought, but felt his heart rate escalate as the weight of this moment pressed upon him.

"I don't know what you are you talking about..."

His pursed lips dropped at the corners, again creating incongruity in the image of his face. Had they failed...again?

"Are you trying to tell me that there are two planes of existence?" Clara's hip turned outward in a stance of opposition. Her head dipped lower, eyes turned up, awaiting a counter-argument. "Who am I? Do I have a family? And what is all *this*?"

He exhaled sharply, turned away and looked off into the distance, then faced her again. "I'm sorry. Let me start over."

Her expression was that of a lost child.

"I know that you can't remember where you came from, but you know that you have a past. This aspect of your existence makes it not only difficult for you, but nearly impossible for me. As disconcerting as that is, you feel oddly comfortable, and you know that what I say is the truth. We *are* at war."

She nodded slowly, accepting what he said, though not knowing why she should. Her hand moved to her temple in an attempt to reconnect.

"You taught Sunday school in your other life, and although the specific memories of the classroom are no longer reachable, the lessons remain." With a nod, he continued: "What do you recall of Genesis?" He was taking a chance, discussing the other life, but he knew no other way.

"Which part? Adam and Eve?" She looked to him for confirmation but still had no understanding. It was as if her mind was simply a search engine, recalling information as it was summoned.

"Yes, yes," he answered. He had found a starting point. "From the beginning, there was always good and evil. The Jewish and Christian faiths share the tale of which you are speaking. Islam teaches that doing good and staying away from evil brings us closer to God. The Buddhist concept of the 'oneness of good and evil' expresses that good and evil are inseparable aspects of life. All religions teach us to triumph over evil. Evil is tangible, and it has many faces. And those faces look no different than yours or mine."

"But what does this have to do with me?"

"It's difficult to explain that part." He gestured with his hands to all that surrounded them, but Clara saw only a kaleidoscope of colors. "For a time, you will waver between your world and mine. We will talk, and meet with others who are reborn for the same purpose. You will gradually forget the details of your other life, and you will come to embrace the lessons that have brought you here. You will be ready."

Clara tilted her head to the side to catch his gaze once more. "I will die."

"It's the only way."

"Who are you?"

"You can call me Elpis."

CHAPTER TWO

"Sweetheart, I know it hurts. I wish I could take it from you. If I could pull that junk out of your body and put it inside me, I would. I swear I would." Tears held back for too long spilled over the young mother's face. Her body wrapped around her little boy, both barely fitting on the small hospital bed.

"No, Mommy. No. I don't want you to feel this." The little boy didn't open his eyes as the words spilled out with little thought. He meant them. The pain was making it hard to focus. Television, games, books...nothing could take his mind off of it all. But he knew his mother was trying. The sound of her voice had always been a comfort to him, even when he shook with fear of his father, or from wandering, or from illness. She was his touchstone, the only thing that really mattered to him. It kept him anchored in this world. He pulled his mother's arms more tightly around his fragile frame, focusing on the constant beeping that had become the soundtrack to his life.

"How can you be so brave, Tommy?" She held her son tightly, no longer afraid of making the pain worse. Forcing away the abhorrent reality, Adira pulled her son against her stomach, feeling only bones beneath his thin skin. Closing her eyes, her motherly dreams transported her to a time when she and he had existed as one. His small movements under her own skin had been momentary reminders of the life within her, so dependent on her every action. It was her decisions and her power that controlled that life. She sheltered him. She protected and fed him. He needed only her for his survival.

Now that power was no longer in her hands.

She tried to remember the clean, powdery smell that attaches itself to all little ones. It reminds parents of the child's purity and calms them, even throughout the craze of sleep deprivation. Baby odors are like smelling salts for parents. And then the child grows older and the powder scent is replaced by the smell of the outdoors. Like the first rainstorms of spring, Adira recalled thinking, when her son would come inside after playing.

But now, as she inhaled Tommy's scent, she could detect nothing that defined *him*. His scent had been replaced with a medicinal odor that reminded her of chemicals. Because cancer has its own smell, and the more pervasive the tumors become, the more pungent the odor. As the cancer cells multiply, the body begins to take on the odor of decayed flowers. The scent can linger for weeks, sometimes months. After the man in 24C had died, Adira had heard the nurses talking about it in quiet tones, trying to determine the best course of action for "freshening" the room before a new patient arrived.

The words formed in her mind more frequently now: *God, take him. If the alternative is suffering here with me, I can't possibly be that selfish. You must need him more than I. Why are You doing this? Please, just take him!*

As the boy's breathing, though labored, began to even out in sleep, the mother looked at her son; not blinking for fear that it might be her last image of him. She brushed her fingers over the ridges of his brow, no longer covered by hair.

It was a habit she had instituted that first night with him in a hospital more than eight years ago. It had been nothing like this day. That joy and adoration had now been replaced with fear and angst. Adira had felt the worries that any new mother experiences when in a hospital room during that first night alone with a newborn. Hardly sleeping, she'd checked again and again to see that he was breathing. Knowing she should leave him to sleep on his own in the clear plastic cradle next to her bed, she couldn't help wanting to pull him into her arms. After a lengthy labor and a few broken blood vessels, she felt ill-prepared for the emptiness she felt now that he was on his own. They had been partners, depending on one another to make it through the arduous months on bed rest. It was also a reprieve from a husband whose drunken rages were his way of laying blame on her for every shortcoming in his own existence. Yet once they had found out about the pregnancy, he had made promises to get help, to be the man that Adira so desperately needed. And so began the first time that Tommy had saved her life.

But, it wouldn't be the last.

Now, here she was, eight years later, watching the twitch of his cheeks as she knew he fought the pain that never seemed to subside. She loved him. More than she had ever loved anything. He had taught her to love, to be good; truly decent.

"Mommy, are there kids in the world who don't have toys?" Even at four years old, his precocious thoughts drove him.

"Yes, unfortunately, yes." Adira had replied, slightly caught off guard by his query.

"Then, we can give my toys to them. I don't need them as much as they do." Tommy's outstretched hand opened to reveal the small red car that was his favorite, one of only a few toys that Adira had been able to provide during all their running. He had never known excess and never would. But even with so little, he taught her that it had been enough.

He believed in her and pushed her to find more in her life than just being a single mother pooling together enough cash to pay rent, let alone medical bills. She had a career because of this little eight-year-old boy. They were both alive because of this dying child. He had been an old soul from the moment he could speak.

Tommy would stop crashing his cars together, notice the faraway look in Adira's eyes and curl up in her lap, putting both hands on her face and say, "I love you, Mommy." There was no better medicine than that. Like a shot of adrenaline, those were the times that strengthened her. It was an amazing thing, being a mother.

God, promise me you have a plan. I never believed in the dogma that the church taught us; how could I? But I always believed in You. Tell me that you are doing this for a reason, because right now, all I want to do is hate You.

CHAPTER THREE

"Υιαγιά, I brought the kids to see you. How are you?"

Clara was dressed in a powder blue track suit; faded stains ran down the front. Her hair splayed at all angles. She looked up from her table absently. It almost appeared that the name, meaning 'grandma' in Greek, no longer registered as something that referred to her. Not sure that Clara had heard her, Elaina hesitated to see if there would be any spark of acknowledgment today. Most days Υιαγιά was able to fake recognition of Elaina. Ironically, it was the word ' Υιαγιά' that seemed to illicit that response. Sometimes she would look at her granddaughter as if she was familiar, maybe even family, but not precisely clear to whom she belonged. On certain days it was clear that until Elaina used her title of γιαγιά, no recognition would come.

Occasionally Clara thought Elaina was her daughter; their appearances *were* similar. Clara would feign conversation with *how are you* or *the weather is very nice today*. And then with a click, she would either reset to start the same conversation again or register her granddaughter's existence anew. Her great-grandchildren, however, were another story. Rarely did Clara recognize them, but

15

frequently their presence softened her. She had always loved children, no matter to whom they belonged. Elaina often brought hers thinking their abundant joy and abandon fought a fraction of Clara's daily internal struggle.

That track suit brought back memories for Elaina. As a girl she would often spend the night at γιαγιά and Παππούς' house, where they would spoil her incessantly and give her stability during a tumultuous adolescent time. Even before that, she had been sitting on the stairs playing with dolls when her grandfather spryly hopped over them and into the foyer. At the same time, he snapped a hand against Clara's behind, forcing a yelp out of the surprised woman's lips. Elaina had laughed, innocently thinking it was silly that γιαγιά was still surprised by it when it happened so often. Her grandparents laughed together as Elaina watched, only in hindsight, understanding the friendship that partnered in true love.

"Παππούς, where are you going?" Elaina had asked her grandfather as he lifted the keys from the hallway table.

Clara sat with her granddaughter, picking up a doll to play and resting her other hand lovingly on Elaina's head. Παππούς answered, "I have a quick meeting. Someone needs a little help, just as we all do some days. Can't you see the big 'S' poking through my shirt?" he pointed to his chest as he spoke, a smile spreading wide across his face. His bright eyes were always a mix of love and mischief. "I'll be back before you're done playing so we can eat dinner. My woman can cook for us and I will be the entertainment." He laughed boisterously as he pounded his chest and gave Υιαγιά's hair a little yank. He was always speaking with silly accents or uproariously laughing to make others smile.

He kissed his women on their heads and slipped quietly out the front door. Elaina never asked what he meant when he would 'help people' but she pictured him as a superhero, sweeping in to save cats in trees or round up some burglars. Later she would learn that he had struggled with alcoholism, but after turning his life around, made it his mission to do the same for others. At his funeral, Elaina had been bombarded with strangers, longing to share their stories about their savior, her Παππούς.

"Mommy, watch what I can do," cried Elaina's four-year-old son, spiraling her back from the warmth of her past to the chill of this reality. Her son drew his feet up to his ears in an amazing display of flexibility that constantly awed his mother. "Hello? Hi, Γιαγιά Clara. How are you?" A smile exploded on his perfect face as he looked to the woman eighty years his senior. "I'm calling you on my foot phone. See?"

"I don't know how you do that, Dre," his mother chuckled as she tickled his now exposed belly. His love blanketed the cool air she fought that day.

In a rare burst of laughter, Clara motioned for her great grandson to come closer to her. The magic of childhood warmed her as well. He obliged, as always, hopping up from his yoga invention to embrace his great γιαγιά. "Αγούδημου, my boy. Σε αγαπω. I love you." She hadn't yet deteriorated to the point where long term memories, like language, escaped her.

Elaina smiled while holding her daughter hoping the moment would sustain itself and somehow, some miracle would allow Clara to remember it and carry it with her.

But it wouldn't last. After changing her daughter and then tossing the dirty diaper in the trash, Elaina returned to find her children playing, but her grandma had slipped away. Helplessly, she watched her grandmother breathe in and out, blink occasionally, remember how to keep her body functioning on this plane of existence. However, she wasn't there. Her eyes had clouded, her mind had lapsed. *Where had she gone?*

These were the moments that scared Elaina the most. Really, she worried for her children. What would they think? How could she explain this to them? She often struggled to determine whether it was right or wrong to bring them here. What good, if any, was she doing by continuing to visit a woman who no longer recognized her and who, in turn, bore less and less resemblance to the grandmother she had known and loved all her life? Sometimes it seemed easier and maybe even best to just take the children and walk away.

God, don't let the kids understand that she isn't really here. Let them play. Let them stay innocent, bathing in the purity of childhood for a little longer. Death is so much easier to understand than this. Death means Heaven to them. It means redemption for the faithful. It means perfection after the challenges of life. It doesn't mean this...this torture. Why would You make people endure this? What did she do to deserve this? How dare You bend her mind to crack it.

CHAPTER FOUR

"*A* bombing at a German bakery in Puna, India kills 10 and injures 60 more. This is the second bombing this year indicating that terrorist cell existence has not dissipated. The first attack was a little over a month ago when a suicide car bomb detonated at a volleyball tournament in Lakki Marwat, Pakistan, killing 105 and injuring 100 more. Terrorist attacks like this have increased since..."

"Turn that off, please! He doesn't need to listen to the troubles of the world while he's grasping for what little peace he gets." Adira watched her son sleep, deep blue-purple circles bled down from her eyes. She hadn't slept in weeks. Not since he came back here. Tommy was her little man. But, looking at him now, she couldn't deny that he was just her small child, beaten down by a disease he hadn't deserved.

He looks so tiny in that bed, she thought to herself, following the needle in his arm up to her last hope for him. Adira knew the chemotherapy was experimental. She was told the odds. She knew. She didn't want to accept it, but she knew. He hadn't spoken to her since the night prior and she was plagued with the hope that he would just slip away somewhere between the then and now. She just couldn't watch him writhe in pain any longer. No mother should ever have to watch the tears pool in the corners of her little boy's eyes as the agony and nausea edged past bearable. No mother should have to watch her son waste away a pound at a time, sinking away from her energetic child to be replaced by another layer of blanket over a cancer ridden body.

"Adira, sweetheart, you needn't stay here tonight. Get some sleep. I will stay with him until you come back."

"Mom, thank you, but no. I'm not leaving him."

"And I'm not leaving you," the other mother grasped Adira's hand sending strength signals through her arm. Her persistence in support came with an unspoken understanding that they wouldn't leave one another again. It had been a long road back to mother and daughter.

Looking back at her son once more, Adira could see that although his small frame stilled to an eerie freeze, his eyes rapidly jumped from side to side beneath their lids. She brushed a hand down her brown hair, overgrown and swept back for convenience, not fashion. Her clothes hung on her, framing the missed meals and incessant stress. They wore her, just as frequently as she'd donned those jeans.

She recalled the phone conversation from the hospital when Tommy had been born. She hadn't spoken to her mother in years. It pained her even now to admit the length. But worse, it pained her to admit the reason.

Tommy's father had convinced her to leave, stressing that they could never be together with *the wicked witch constantly meddling in our business.*

Adira had been young, and at the time, thought she was in love.

She had been wrong.

But she admitted it that day when Tommy was born. Looking into his baby slate eyes, she knew that no mother could ever willingly abandon their child. She had abandoned her mother. For a man.

"Mom?" she had simply asked through her room phone in the hospital. She squeezed her baby son more for her own comfort and strength than for his, and waited for a response.

"Adira?" she heard the shake in her mother's voice and listened and relaxed her tense shoulders as the New York accent pulled at the vowels in her name. No one said it like her mom. Adeeerrraa.

"Oh, Mom. I'm so sorry. I am so sorry about how I hurt you. Please forgive me. Please..."

"I forgive you." Her mother had said before she could even get the words out.

"I've had a son. Tommy. And he's perfect and beautiful and I want you to meet him and..."

"Where are you?" And that was it. Adira's mother drove halfway across the country to her daughter and brand new grandson and brought them home never looking back at the mistakes of the past.

It was as if they had been someone else's memories.

CHAPTER FIVE

"Ὑιαγιά, don't you know that I would never do anything to hurt you?" The younger woman pushed the already-in-place hair behind her ears again, scratching at the skin beneath in a painful gesture to steady herself. Whistling a breath deeply into her lungs, she fought for composure.

"You all are trying to take my money. Get out! Get the hell out!" The older of the two stared right through her granddaughter. Vacant, but screaming. As if her body and her mind were of separate beings, she sat, unmoving from the neck down. Her head, however, waved back and forth appearing to be controlled awkwardly by a puppeteer.

Clara Eros's family had been making excuses for her behavior for years. But it had only gotten worse. Dementia. Alzheimer's. Call it what you would, but for a family, it was simply hell. Watching a loved one peel away the layers of memory in increments, sometimes bursting with anger and ugliness, is beyond devastating. It debilitates. It preys upon the good memories and replaces them with a darkness that leaves only a shade of the person they now convince themselves they once loved. Until one day, a choice must be made. Do we remember

Γιαγιά as she was before and ignore what she has become? Or let the memory of her former self fade and focus daily on trying to connect with this version of who she has become? It's a constant struggle. One that requires not only patience, but a numbing effect to handle the hurtling abuse.

Signs emerged years earlier when Clara had taken that same granddaughter, Elaina, to Europe for a celebration of Elaina's high school graduation. They were making memories together that would soon be stripped away. It was the anger that Elaina had first noticed. The occasional memory loss had been there. But like most people who are stretched thin by emotion and activity, she began to misplace her keys more frequently or couldn't recall names of acquaintances. These were common, Elaina had thought. Hell, she was seventeen and occasionally forgot what her mom had asked her to buy at the store. That wasn't something to worry about. Was it? After this trip, all moments combined with it and Elaina began to think something was changing in her γιαγιά. Like a cloud, it permeated through the jovial Clara and burst with emotion uncharacteristic of Elaina's grandmother. And that was only the beginning.

"Why the hell are you making me take this train for three hours to see a bunch of rocks?" Clara had stared at her granddaughter, accusation licking the tips of her eyelashes.

"Γιαγιά, it is Stonehenge. You know, one of the great Wonders of the World? How can we be this close and not go and see it?" The seventeen-year-old Elaina had been cognizant of having spoken to her grandmother about this for the months preceding the trip. It hadn't even been just once. It was multiple conversations that lined the planning of this trip. How could she be asking this question now? This was supposed to be their adventure; the trip they had always talked about taking together. They had both been so excited to see "a bunch of rocks." Hadn't they? What had changed?

Yιαγιά had.

"I just think you're ungrateful. You haven't even offered to pay me back for this trip." Clara rubbed her hands through her silver hair, creasing her thinning skin with tension. The silver hair that had been her trademark came undone from its always perfect quaff. Quaking from an emotion Elaina had never seen in her grandmother, she steadied her hands rubbing them back and forth on her legs.

Pay you back for the trip, Elaina had thought. *I'm only seventeen. I'm leaving for college soon. I thought this trip was a gift. I thought this was what you wanted. Where is this coming from? I've thanked you profusely. I feel so lucky to be here. How am I ungrateful? Am I doing something wrong? Have I become one of those spoiled brats I despise? What the hell is going on?* The questions pelted her heart, chipping away at the solidity that had always been their relationship. But still, she had remained silent.

They had spent their time with "the rocks", the train ride back to the hotel and the rest of the evening not speaking, but snarling at one another. Elaina let the tears silently slide her heart into sleep.

The next day, it was as if it had never happened.

But it had. And that niggling feeling that Elaina had done something wrong in the eyes of her perfect γιαγιά ate away at her. That had been fifteen years ago now and only the first of many incidents that would transpose into a deeply concerning sense that something was wrong. The accusations didn't end with Elaina. They slowly extended and wrapped themselves around other family members, too. *She's stealing from me.* She would erupt. *Someone came in here and took my ring!* Her arms would flail. *Why are they doing this to me?* She would weep, calling Elaina, begging for help that she just couldn't give.

And the reactions became more extreme, while the repetition increased and shortened in intervals.

Here Elaina was staring at the same woman, but not her γιαγιά at all. The silver haired beauty, whose mask slipped that day those fifteen years ago, was no longer there. That silver hair had morphed to white, carelessly reaching for the memories that freed themselves from her mind. Her clothes were wrinkled with overuse and under bathing. Where once Elaina had complained about the exotic perfumes Υιαγιά would purchase from around the world, a smell was emanating from her that was reminiscent of mold and stale air, like a cave where artifacts had stagnated over time.

Elaina struggled with conversation. She'd mentally armed herself with topics...her kids, her classroom, events in the city. As the disease had progressed, she'd found that it had become painful to talk with her grandmother. If she allowed silence to breathe around her, the reiteration of idol topics would bounce between them.

Look at those clouds. The sky is so blue... Clara would say with the kids in the car.

Yes, it is. Elaina would respond.

A minute would pass.

The sky is so blue. Look at the clouds.

Elaina had learned to ignore it. She had to. But, it was hard to explain to her little ones, who never understood it when their great γιαγιά would say "*Aren't you going to give me a kiss hello?*" seconds after they had kissed her.

Even so, Clara's family loved her deeply. She had been the one to teach them how to love. Clara had spent years supporting Elaina. Talking to her about boys, her parents, and just being a listening ear when Elaina was at her worst. Their long talks through Elaina's tears, while Clara lovingly scratched her granddaughter's back were memories that kept Elaina securely in this horror, rather than turning her back to run.

Clara had helped people, really helped them. For her entire life, she had supported others, took them into her house, let them stay in her rooms. Giving money to those in need without a second thought, volunteering for church functions, she was the quintessential Υιαγιά. With a minor dose of Greek guilt, she was bursting with love for her family and literally, couldn't get enough of them. *When am I going to see you?* she would ask incessantly. They would joke with each other about it never being enough to see one another as often as they did. And sometimes life got in the way, pushing those visits farther apart. Over the phone, nevertheless, they maintained the same connection. *I love you,* Elaina would say. And Clara would reply, *"I love you more."* But slowly, like a creeping predator, the love began to fade and twist into something dark. "I love you, *γιαγιά,*" Elaina would say in more recent days. "But, not enough to see me," Clara would end with friction rather than love.

It was wearing.

She'd once had her great love in her husband, as well. Like everything else, it had been unconditional...when conditions could have pushed them apart. Clara nursed him through a debilitating fight with lung cancer when most wives would have crumbled. Through years of marriage, children, weddings, grandchildren; they had been strong. Together. And then he was gone. It was the smoking, as Clara had always predicted.

"Do you think I don't know what you are doing down there?" she would yell, a smile forcing itself to the outskirts of her eyes. She knew he was sneaking cigarettes in the basement bathroom again. But, she was defeated in her frustration and loved him too much to hate him for it. As a child, it was like listening to a comedy. Clara was loud and bossy, but percolating with good intentions. He was goofy, always with an easy smile and smack on her backside. But he smoked. And he acted as if they all didn't smell it, and shrugged his shoulders with a nonchalant sparkle to his eye when he'd been caught. There was a point when Elaina had decided he wanted to get caught, but he just couldn't stop. He had tried. For as long as Elaina knew him, those short thirteen years, he had been "trying to quit". And in the end he'd pulled Elaina into an embrace one of the last times that she would see him. His skin was pocked and yellowed from the jaundice. The whites of his eyes marred by a glossy egg yolk. His cold hands wrapped around his granddaughter as he whispered to her, "Never pick up a damn cigarette. Promise me. I was stupid, thinking I was invincible, and I should have listened to Γιαγιά. She's always right, that one. God, I love her. And, I love you. Never forget that."

Theirs was a love that was strong and good. Elaina thought about those times often now, memories like colorful flashes when you're a child. Although Παππούς and Γιαγιά often playfully bickered, there was such love there. Like her Spartan ancestors, Γιαγιά fought unfailingly and protected Παππούς when he got sick. She was with him every step of the way, never allowing the isolation that can come with death. When her famous chocolate milkshakes had turned to liquid food, crushed with protein powders for Παππούς, his strength had waned so desperately that he could no longer eat solid foods. Her hugs had transformed to pulling him from bed and holding him while he relieved himself. And when he apologized profusely for letting her down in death, she refused to make him feel small. Although she dished out as much as she took, she had refused to stop fighting, even when he had.

But now, she was no longer that person.

Where had that fight gone?

CHAPTER SIX

*"T*wo female suicide bombers?" Elpis's voice rang out as he read the report. His dark hair was cut short, as he preferred it. His green eyes, rimmed with unease, rose to his friend.

"It was the peak of rush hour in the Metro."

"How many?"

"Forty."

"It's time." Elpis had decided, but he looked to his friend for confirmation.

"It's too soon. She isn't ready to say goodbye."

"Mothers never are. And they shouldn't have to. But we need him." Elpis dropped his eyes. "He hasn't lived long enough to establish many relationships, especially with those who have passed over. Who should I look like when he arrives?"

"He's a worthy young man. Don't worry about form. In fact, I'll go."

"Then let it begin."

Elpis's robes danced behind him, a relic of a past he now preferred in his sanctuary. He continued to prepare his friend. Andreas would be perfect.

Andreas examined his mentor as he mentally prepared himself for the role reversal. Although robes weren't always the wardrobe of choice, especially when they were training, they served as a reminder of Elpis's veneration. Andreas had never asked him about his own transition, if indeed he had undergone one. It had always been a taboo subject between them. Andreas just assumed that when it was time, Elpis would tell him.

It had been years ago, almost twenty now, when they had first met. It was their first mission together and they were at the helm, coordinating all the players in a dance of destruction and opposition. Positioning themselves as air traffic controllers, they had intercepted the first transmissions amidst the chaos.

"This is Jeremy onboard Oceanair #333. I have one pilot down and at least one target claiming to be strapped with C4. I need an outside visual."

Andreas continued in an unemotional vein. "Target is São Paulo Center. You're going to have to reveal yourself, Jeremy."

"There are sixty-four passengers on board! I can't—"

"You can't save them. But you will save thousands more if you can divert. That's why you're there."

The atoms of Jeremy's phantom image reflected transient light as he moved toward the cockpit.

"We need to increase our numbers," said Elpis.

Andreas slammed his hand on the table forcing papers and photos to bounce. "We only react to what they do. Balance no longer exists. This day is proof of that."

"If we increase our numbers, we risk being recognized." Elpis shook his head, weighing what he knew to be necessary against the effects his actions might have on humanity. "But it's a risk we must take. We don't have a choice."

CHAPTER SEVEN

Blinking viciously, rapidly, eyes adjusting to a new filter, Tommy took in his surroundings. Colors bounced off cement walls reflecting a kaleidoscope of features. People lined as far as he could see, faces unfamiliar to him. Hair, skin and clothes of every hue imaginable; but, no single image sparked recognition.

Is this a subway?

He confirmed tracks running through the center of this sea of people. Jostled by a bump to his shoulder, his reaction was to apologize, but he froze when he stood eye to eye with the man that had run into him.

Am I taller?

His toe crunched over a piece of paper. Thinking how unusual it was that he had heard the crunch over the din of voices echoing through the tunnel, Tommy reached to pick it up, but as his fingertips touched the white sheet, he turned his palms toward his face.

These aren't my hands.

Shaking at the sudden realization, he studied the strange digits. His hands were older now; bigger, stronger. He fisted his fingers, as if testing that strength. Touching thumb to finger, experimenting with the effects of contact, he could feel every nerve, every sensation. Years of chemotherapy and radiation had led the way to burning and numbness in his feet and hands, both of which had become his companions over the last year. Even that day when the Make a Wish Foundation had given him the gift of a trip to Disneyland, he had dropped his light saber because his hands had failed to send the message to his brain to hold tightly.

He moved his fingers up to what he expected to be withered biceps, only to find the muscles had become strong and sinewy bulges. His hands reached for his face, feeling each curve like a person who'd suddenly lost his sight. Quickly, he found the plastic covering of an advertisement board and stared at his foggy reflection to be sure that the person staring back at him was the same person he'd always known.

"Oh my God!" a voice rang out behind him.

Turning, he didn't look for the source of the voice, but rather the reason behind the exclamation. His thoughts seemed to be in overdrive. He stepped away from the advertisement toward the train platform to clear himself of the crowd around him. His height allowed him to see over most of the onlookers in the vicinity from which the commotion originated. He saw a woman dressed in a blue business suit lying on the tracks below. Her teeth were clenched and her torso was shaking in seizure. Without hesitating, he jumped six feet to the rail bed, landing in a crouch to absorb impact. Looking left, he saw a train light approaching.

Grabbing her, he slowed his rapid-fire thoughts and lifted her effortlessly. Her black hair fell limply over his back as he heaved her over his left shoulder. With the train approaching at full speed, he began to hoist the woman's limp body toward the crowd of onlookers, hoping for help. A hand reached out from the masses to pull as he pushed, sliding her over the lip of the platform.

The crowd backed away from the track, now tending to the woman who had fallen. With a powerful jump, Tommy reached for the platform just as the helpful Samaritan took his arm. At first, his fingers met only air, although he could see the hand reaching toward him. Upon a second try, the same fingers met flesh. Employing all their strength, they pulled and lifted, and both men tumbled onto the platform. Breathless, they watched with wide eyes as the train slowed. As it came to a stop, the woman woke from her seizure.

Overwhelmed by unanswered questions, Tommy jumped to his feet and raced toward the closest exit avoiding attention. Footsteps followed him. As he emerged from the subway entrance, he allowed himself a peek behind.

"Tommy? Or perhaps we should call you Tom now..."

"I don't understand," he stammered.

"You will..."

"Where am I? And how do you know my name?"

"All your questions will be answered in good time."

"Who are you?"

"I am Andreas."

CHAPTER EIGHT

Seventy-five thoughts and seventy-five prayers.
A savior emerged amongst the broken glass.
To pull out of harm, the beautiful lass.
He left no name, no return address,
Just did what mattered under all duress.
Risking life, limb and family,
He returned the young lady from reverie.
Amazing that only a single soul from that seventy-five
Chose to do the impossible and kept her alive.
It's moments like that we should document
Rather than hatred in new forms we invent.

"Υιαγιά, did you hear that news story about the guy who pulled a woman from a subway tunnel? She'd had a seizure and fell onto the tracks. Can you believe it? Seriously, I thought these things only happened in movies. But, that's not the worst part. No one did a thing. That subway station must have been packed at that time of day. They estimated seventy-five, but it had to have been closer to one hundred. Save for one guy. Some unidentified man just jumped down there." Elaina felt her throat clog with emotion that she didn't know existed for a man she'd never met. "He got her out, too. Then just bolted. He didn't need fame or recognition or even a thank you. He just did what was right and walked away. How many people could do that? Of course the media is creating speculation that he has something to hide. Anyway, I wrote this poem to use with my students and it just reminded me of being a teenager full of angst sitting at that kitchen table, reading you my ridiculous poetry." She stared at the now empty table, green chairs like soldiers protecting its memories. Elaina's eyes drifted back to her grandmother whose focus was somewhere far away. " Γιαγιά?"

Clara didn't respond. Or maybe she couldn't. Her breaths came in and out with consistency, but her brain wore away.

You always listened, Elaina thought, *so I will stay here and listen for you.*

"Elpis, when will it end for me? On the other side, I mean. Am I hurting the people around me by hanging on like this? Why can't I just remain here?" Clara knew her line of questioning was almost childlike, but through her understanding of the cause she had also become invigorated by her responsibility even though she felt uneasy about the part of herself she could not recall.

"Clara, you know that there are effects for every cause, and balance is what this is all about." Elpis studied the histories laid out before him. He'd committed them to memory, of course, but with each recruit it was like looking at the world through brand new eyes. "You've seen the symbols of yin and yang, am I correct?"

Clara nodded in recognition, feeling triumphant with each recollection.

"Do you remember our last conversation, when we spoke of good and evil and the Garden of Eden?"

"Yes."

Elpis reached across the boardroom table strewn with dusty volumes, papers and tablets lying in organized chaos and found a black leather-bound book. Instantly, he was able to open it to a page in the middle with a picture as its focus. "Have you ever seen this? It's Michelangelo's painting of the sin of Adam and Eve from the ceiling of the Sistine Chapel. What do you notice about the people in the painting?"

"They're naked." Silliness made her feel normal, but it wasn't her place to by silly.

"Well, yes," Elpis answered with a smile. "Notice that one of the couples is facing toward the serpent while the other couple is facing away from it. This symbolizes the internal struggle between submitting to temptation and avoiding it."

Clara looked again at the picture, thinking she must never have been very good at seeing the unseen. "Still seeing naked people..." Even in the short time that she had spent with Elpis, she enjoyed teasing him. It made her feel real, when much of her did not.

"Glad to know the fate of what is good in this world is in the hands of such an observant woman." Elpis studied her, the physical form that she had become. She was now strong and graceful. The chestnut and red tones of her affluent hair had replaced the brittle gray matte that disease had imposed. The lines around her eyes creased now in thoughts or laughter, instead of conspiring to hide the person she once was. Alzheimer's had trapped her, but finally she had emerged from her cocoon.

"What does that picture of the swinging couples have to do with yin and yang?"

"Good question. Thank you for bringing me back to my point. The yin and yang originated as a Taoist visual symbol—"

Clara interrupted. "It has become much more than that today, don't you think?"

"Yes, of course. However, you know the two tear-drop

shaped halves where one half is black and the other is white. The black half has a small white circle in it, while the white half has a black one."

"I know what the yin and yang symbol looks like. It's the Taoist reference where you lost me." Clara swept her curls away from her face.

"Taosim, modernly known as Daoism, is a philosophical and religious tradition that originated in China. The yin and yang is a cyclical theory of becoming and dissolution. It is a theory on the interdependence between the world of nature and human events. It's all about balance. As you so eloquently put it, the 'swingers' in Michelangelo's painting represent two couples: one that accepts sin and one that does not accept it. The implied balance exists both mathematically in the number and conceptually in the idea. One cannot understand that something is good without the existence of evil. We live in a dualistic world of delicately balanced, and often opposing, forces. Yin and yang originated with a belief that through balance, harmony can be attained in the world. The symbol reflects light and dark, night and day. The cycle is never ending. Birth and death remain the greatest balance."

Clara nodded as Elpis continued.

"I always felt that Shih-tou's poem explained it most clearly." Elpis scattered more papers and books around the table, searching for a particular volume.

"*The Identity of Relative and Absolute*," Clara looked up as she read the title aloud.

> *Within the light there is darkness,*
> *But do not try to understand the darkness.*
> *Within darkness there is light,*
> *But do not look for that light.*
> *Light and darkness are a pair,*
> *Like the foot before and the foot behind in walking.*
> *Each thing has its own intrinsic value*

And is related to everything else in function and position.
Ordinary life fits the absolute as a box and its lid.
The absolute works together with the relative,
Like two arrows meeting in mid-air.

Scratching an itch that didn't exist behind her ear, Clara quietly reflected on the words before her. "I like the box and its lid, because a box isn't complete without a lid. I think I get the concept of everything being relative. In other words, I wouldn't know what pain was if I was in a constant state of pain. I can only feel pain because I know what it is like to feel no pain. Men and women are interdependent opposites, too, right?" She raised her head in question, beginning to wrap her mind around the concept.

"Exactly!" Elpis was energized by Clara's understanding. Excitedly, he stood taller, gesticulating grandly. "It's all about perspective. You may feel the high of winning, but you need to remember that for you to have attained that win, you in turn removed it from someone else."

"Okay, I think I'm starting to get it. But what does this have to do with why I'm here?" Finally she was taking ownership of her lessons but now she wanted a purpose. Although she couldn't remember, she knew she was slowly wasting away in another place and time, and there were people around who seemed to be suffering all the more for these lessons she was learning here. She didn't need to remember them specifically to know it was truly happening.

"There is no God and there is no Devi—at least not as we think of Zeus and Hades—no two entities battling for all eternity against one another. It is more like the Alpha and the Omega. One force balancing with another. Over the centuries, we have provided guidance to humans, but we have never removed their ability to choose. For as often as we have tried to guide toward the good, the

Poneros have guided the Athoos toward evil."

Elpis met Clara's eyes just as she asked, "Innocent?"

"Yes, the Athoos or 'innocent' is how we refer to the human population that remains unaware of our existence, and thus vulnerable to the influence of the Poneros." Elpis hesitated for a moment. "One can't pick them out from the general population. The only times we are able to identify someone consumed by the Poneros is during the seconds before a horrific choice. The Poneros are systematic and calculating, with a proclivity toward evil that seems to be innate. It isn't something tangible. There are some people who just want to watch the world incinerate." Elpis shook his head, looking away from Clara's horrified expression. "We can't actually fight against them; we can only try to maintain the balance. If we fail, the world *will* be destroyed."

"I've always believed that good would prevail over evil..."

"A nice thought, but the Athoos tend to sensationalize horror and minimize heroism. The Poneros thrive on weak moments and optimize opportunities to fracture human nature. What better way to divide people than to make them hate each other?"

"The Poneros can do that?"

"Sometimes, but they also can't control the love that people feel for one another."

A knock on the door interrupted Elpis. "What is it?" he asked as he acknowledged the messenger.

"It appears that they've hit again," he said in a calm yet serious voice. For that small moment, Clara saw the same inconsistency in his image that she had thought she'd seen the first time they'd met.

"And so the balance shall be maintained," he pronounced.

CHAPTER NINE

$\mathcal{A}$dira's tears had been drained months ago and now she stood in front of a photograph resting on the small box that held her child. She laid her hand upon the lid, staring at the picture she had chosen for the simple silver frame. She sang to herself and to the picture:

> *You are my one and only*
> *My Tommy through and through*
> *forever and always*
> *my love for you is true.*

She had tried to choose a picture taken before Tommy had become sick, but it now seemed as if that time had never existed. Even in the picture, the rims of his cyanotic eyes portended the onset of disease. Yet his face showed joy as he looked not at the camera, but at a dog that had run across his field of vision. His dark eyelashes contrasted his white skin. The stubborn cowlick at the crown of his head reminded her how she'd loved to run her fingers through his fine hair. He'd rarely cried as a baby and more often than not had comforted her during her daily struggles. Feeling pressure building in her throat, she turned toward the black-clad people behind her. In a haze of emotion, she walked past her memories of Tommy, seeing faces and recalling emotions, though precise connections seemed curiously obscure.

She made her way to a chair positioned at the back of the room. Tears of frustration and pain and anger spilled out in a torrent.

Her mother approached her as she rubbed the streaks away from her face. "You're looking at me strangely," she said.

"Sorry, I'm not..."

"You're not yourself," her mother finished. "Tommy took something from you and I don't know if you can ever have it back."

Adira let herself cry again, this time upon her mother's shoulder, not caring who heard as the sobs racked her body.

> *You are my one and only*
> *My Tommy through and through*
> *forever and always*
> *my love for you is true.*

"He *will* always be your baby, just as you will always be mine. We'll lean on each other." Her mother's singing rang through her as she thought of her son and missed him with every fiber of her being.

CHAPTER TEN

"*H*ow do you know who I am?"

Andreas looked at the man standing before him. "This is who you are now."

Tommy's new face flushed with frustration, reminding Andreas of the intense emotions that affixed themselves to such a dramatic transition.

"I was in the subway, sent there to meet you in order to help you understand the transition."

"What transition?"

Andreas laid his hand on Tommy's shoulder. "Your mother was right; you are an old soul."

"Do you know my mother?" The pain of her memory pierced his new body like freezing rain.

"I'm like you," Andreas related. "I had cancer." The words floated out in what seemed like an echo. "I died."

"Am I dead?"

"That is what I'm about to explain to you. I think you will comprehend more quickly than most."

Tommy pulled at the corner of his shirt in a child's gesture that seemed out of place on a young man's body. "What am I now? I don't look like me, I don't feel like me, but I remember who I was, who I left behind. And I remember dying..."

"Okay, let's talk about you physically. You were an eight-year-old cancer victim in your other life, but here you are in your prime." Andreas stopped at Tommy's addled look.

"Why me?"

"The big guy picked you." Andreas gestured overhead as he spoke. "He chooses people who are innately and unfalteringly good. Unfortunately, he also allows the cancer to spread. In order for us to become like this, our bodies must first be broken down. What easier way to do that than a cancer cell that already inhabits all human bodies? The potential for cancer not only exists in every cell of the body, but it also supports that cell's growth and health. Everyone has it and everyone has just the same ability to acquire cancer, as we did. It is a delicate balance." Andreas paused to wait for the questions he knew were coming.

"How old were you when you had...when you...died?" Tommy asked.

Looking him straight in the eye, Andreas answered honestly. "I was sixty-six. I had lived a full life. I was lucky enough to know love. I also had two beautiful daughters. I got to meet my two grandchildren. You didn't get any of that. For that, I'm sorry. But you've been given a second chance. You have a new life now, and although it may not be quite what you thought your first life would be, you can still make something useful and noble of it. Your body has been restored...for a different purpose."

Tommy allowed himself to think of his mother. He envisioned her hair and the flecks of green in her hazel eyes. He saw the gray strands of age that had begun painting her head, more prolific as his hospital stays lengthened. He thought of the song she used to sing to him when he was in pain. He thought of her dreams to watch him graduate, to fall in love, or find a career. All those dreams she'd had for him when they still had hope. But in time even hope had faded.

Tommy's eyes returned to Andreas.

"You will miss her and she will miss you. Love never fades away, but the sadness does. She will be okay. I think there is a part of us that breaks watching people we love suffer, and it can only be fixed when the suffering ends. For her, your suffering has ended. There is peace in that."

"Will I ever see her again?"

"That's a question that cannot be answered. But you can have faith. And it's okay to be happy, because you will be happy again. There are benefits to this life; embrace them."

"What do you mean by 'a different purpose?'"

"You are one of many who make up the Go'El. I am one too. We fight against the Poneros." He stopped for a moment, knowing that he was literally speaking another language. He thought about how he could make Tommy understand. Abruptly, it came to him. "What is the most awful thing that you have ever witnessed?"

"My dad," Tommy responded without hesitation. "He used to hit my mom and me. Nothing is worse than someone turning on the people who love them."

"And that is what you will be fighting against," said Andreas.

CHAPTER ELEVEN

"What happened? Where did she go?" Andreas was confused.

"She wasn't ready."

"What do you mean she wasn't ready?" Andreas tried to tamp down his escalating anxiety.

"She has to let go of what's behind her. The process isn't complete. But she's close." Elpis put a hand out, gesturing for his friend to take the seat that was still warm from Clara's recent presence.

Elpis propelled through each piece of information on the tablet Andreas had brought to him, efficiently taking it all in. "Most people think that a clean slate would be refreshing, but having intelligence without emotions, and no memories or context—that is painful."

Elpis struggled to remain stoic in the presence of his friend. There was still so much to be done. And there was the mission.

"Okay, what's the game plan?"

"Two people have already been confirmed dead. The shooter is still moving and unidentified. Classes started minutes ago. They haven't even had a warning."

"Let's go!"

"Ὑιαγιά, did you read this already?" Elaina pointed to the open newspaper on the table, knowing that her grandmother loved to read it front to finish each day. It was one of the reasons it had been so shocking the first time they had learned of the illness. She had always kept her mind so sharp. She had never been a dull-minded or passive person. How could this be happening to her?

Yet she was always distracted these days. The times when she faded to gray had become more frequent and lasted longer.

"I don't know. What day is it?" Clara responded, but didn't seem to care for a response. Or maybe she hadn't remembered that she'd asked the question. The amount of time that Clara "engaged" during the day had become extremely limited. It had reached a point where during Elaina's visits, sometimes Clara did not acknowledge her at all. Still, Elaina returned.

Elaina's eyes drifted back to the article that lay in front of her. As a teacher, as a mother, as a person, it was hard not to feel emotional about the words on the page. The dark stain of a tear connected each word as she read.

> "...the professor was 76 years old and had survived the Holocaust. He was shot by the Virginia Tech assailant while barricading his classroom door in order to save his students. The task for which he set out was accomplished with honor. He single-handedly saved the lives of several students, while sacrificing his own."

Sirens roared and lights flashed creating a desperate cacophony and a rainbow of primary colors in an atmosphere of suffering and pain.

"What is the point of all this? We've been increasing our numbers and recruiting advisors so that we can anticipate these attacks. Is this balance?" Andreas gracelessly gestured to the students and teachers surrounding him. Thirty-two had suffered at the hands of the Poneros before he'd taken his own life.

"It is new to recruit the advisors, and we only have one in training. There is no way to anticipate these attacks, and there is no way to end them." Elpis concentrated in order to clasp his friend's shoulder as a reminder of what they were working toward. He knew this would be difficult for Andreas. He knew his emotions were raw. "There is no life without pain. And it's awful. It sometimes makes me question my role. But then I remember those we save. There is power in that. We have to hold on to salvation. Being first to the fight is never the answer."

"We lost a fighter today." Andreas looked at the white sheets that covered the massacred victims. "He was my trainer. I met him soon after my transition. He faced the greatest symbol of malevolence the world has ever seen. And he was there, living in a concentration camp as a child. And now he had to face it again. He did what was necessary and right and good. And he did it with courage, I know."

Elpis looked from the sheets back to Andreas and recalled his interactions with The Professor, as they all fondly called him. "The face of the Poneros is changing, just as we are. It used to be that we would look for the swastika, the straight arm held out in reverence toward a master with a discernable face and presence. It was a ridiculous mustache." He said the last part almost to himself, reminding Andreas that he had been there too, in his time, in his own way. He had been face to face with Hitler. It wasn't just a horror story written in history books to scare people into empathy. "He recruited children first. He knew what creating his youth leaders would do for a culture. It was cruel and calculating. The Poneros optimized that. Children are malleable. Do you think Mao didn't do the same? Stalin? And now the Lord's Resistance Army in South Sudan? The Poneros are not stupid; never underestimate the sick intelligence behind annihilation.

Look at the genocides that are happening today. Children are forced to run all night long, lock themselves in cages and pray for redemption. If not, they are taken from their beds, forced into servitude and brainwashed to kill their families. But, still the Poneros had a face. They had a leader." Andreas stopped long enough to point to the picture on the screen inside the squad car. "The face of evil is no longer just a man willing to force the changes the Poneros have orchestrated. It's no longer a child brought up to believe that the devastation of the world is right. No, that is what scares me. The Poneros no longer have a face, a rhyme, or a reason. It strikes anywhere, any time. And it definitely struck here today. That's why it is Clara's time. You're right, we need more than fighters. We need to evolve, just as they have evolved. They played their queen today in this chess game. It's time we start planning to play ours."

CHAPTER TWELVE

Tom had gathered with some of the others who had been called in too late after the devastating events of the day. The discussion after the massacre at the university took a philosophical turn. How could they not analyze the reasons behind what had happened and why they were there? It had been Tom's first mission. He had felt useless since his only job had been to report in only after the attack had ended.

That helplessness was not a feeling, he learned, that he alone harbored. The others in the group were all fairly new recruits, although he was the least experienced.

"Elpis worries about us," Tahrim explained. Tom looked to her as if she had been reading his mind. Her smile was meant to comfort, but he could see wariness behind her eyes that he had not seen before this day. It had been one of loss. That feeling could not be swept away easily.

The silence settled around them in expectation of Tahrim's explanation. As he waited, Tom found a patience settling within him that he hadn't experienced since his arrival. His eyes scanned the trees that surrounded them.

At this time of dusk, the light played tricks, allowing the housing in which they lived to settle into shadows.

Tahrim's words unsettled him. "Athoos only see what they want to see. Today, the cloud of horror was too much for them. They could only hear those stories. Shake their heads. Change their channels. Once they make their decisions, they cannot see anything else."

They were settled on the ground, pulling warmth from the fire that Tom had made. They sat together, allowing time to settle the adrenaline. "It is easy for us to find places to train, and to live. Athoos are physically limited, where we are not, of course."

"How long have you been with the Go'El?" Tom asked her.

"About eight months." She gathered her thick chestnut hair and held it above her head. "My first mission was in Germany: two suitcase bombs. Andreas was the one that stopped them. I was just called in to write the reports afterward. I'm thankful that my first assignment was to follow up a success. They are rare." She looked to Tom, who had been tracing lines in the dirt to his side with a stick.

"There is a story about the Prophet Muhammad. Each day, he would walk past an old woman who would throw trash at him, scorning his message. Each day, he continued to walk the same path; she continued to throw her trash. And each day, he showed patience. No malice. Until one day, the woman was not there. The Prophet asked about her and found that she had taken ill. The Prophet immediately went to visit her. When she questioned why he was there, he simply responded that Allah teaches him that if someone is sick, a Muslim should seek him out and try to help."

Once again, the silence settled around them, nothing but wind chasing through the trees. "My mother once told me a story when I asked her about religion," Tom told his new friends. "During the first century, a great rabbi named

Hillel was asked to define Judaism while standing on one foot. He replied, 'Certainly! What is hateful to you, do not do to your neighbor. That is the Torah. The rest is just commentary, now go and study.'"

Tom smiled in memory of that anecdote and waited for his compatriots to comment. Some, like him, were Jewish, although he had never really felt the meaning behind that label since he and his mom had claimed the religion only in name rather than in practice. Other newly established friendships were with those who claimed Christianity or Islam as their faiths, and there were even some who embraced polytheism. Together they compared the religions, not to prove one perspective correct over the other, but to define the common threads that now brought them together.

"That story stuck with me. I always liked its simplicity. I don't believe that God deals in absolutes."

"What do you mean by 'absolutes'?" Banko, a young woman of the Buddhist faith, said quietly after listening to Tom's story. "There are absolutely evil actions, are there not?" She looked not directly at Tom, but her words penetrated, nonetheless.

"Today was absolutely evil, yes." Tom bit out the words, his once subsided anger surfacing again.

"Buddhism does not see good and evil as separate elements, or absolutes, in the way to which you may be referring. But those two are relational. There is good and evil in an act, and the impact of that act on your life and the lives of others. Evil actions are rooted in selfishness. We must stand up to that evil when it comes. 'One who is thoroughly awakened to the nature of good and evil from their roots to their branches and leaves is called a Buddha.' Buddhism teaches us to walk the path of life with an inner contentment, and to abandon that which causes or leads to harm and suffering. I know that I am here to counter that suffering. And I am ready."

CHAPTER THIRTEEN

"We've intercepted an e-mail between a civilian and a senior recruiter for a terrorist group. This recruiter has been involved in planning terrorist operations for the last several years. Seven days ago he entered a gun manufacturing facility and purchased a FN five-seven semi-automatic. He's been shooting at various ranges during the past six days and is getting pretty accurate at shredding those silhouette targets at about one hundred yards." Elpis shared the information with Andreas and Tom, allowing them time to study the evidence. Tom had become Andreas's shadow, but he was emerging as a leader.

"Why haven't we gone in sooner?" Andreas slid his finger from one screen to the next.

"You know how this goes, Andreas. We have to be sure. There is no room for mistakes."

"We can't always act defensively. Sooner or later, we'll have to pre-empt." Andreas's voice was confident, not sharp.

Elpis knew how he felt. He himself had once thought that eliminating a target was the best means of prevention. It meant saving lives. But he now understood that taking a life was neither the only nor the best option. He looked from Andreas to Tom, who was still staring at the photo on the screen. *This is your first. Are you ready?* His thoughts betrayed him as the concern reflected back into Tom's stare.

"I'm ready. It's my time, now." Tom related with a look of utter determination.

"Okay, I think you two should have a little chat with our boy, here." Upon first try, Elpis's finger moved through his screen. With a roll of his neck, he tapped the picture again with more conviction sending the photo and location to the other men's devices.

They had started Tom's training months ago. More than a year now, in all. Tom had wondered what training would be like. His father had been in the military long before he'd met his mother, so Tom had heard stories.

They weren't pretty.

He understood that there needed to be a level of physical and emotional toughness that instilled harmony between insanity and heroism. Let's be honest, he'd thought, you'd have to be a little bit crazy to run in front of a line of bullets.

Tom wasn't crazy, but he had a lot to learn about this new existence.

"What are my limitations?" he had asked Andreas on his way to his first training session. "I mean, are we impenetrable?" He rubbed his hands instinctively along the biceps that still felt new to him.

"I will show you," Andreas responded with a smirk.

Located in the heart of Yellowstone, the training facility was the only part of their compound that spread its fingers into an area that was even remotely affected by the human population. Located partially under the western edge of the Shoshone Lake, the facility occupied the Caldera of a dormant volcano. The Go'El referred to it adoringly as "the pot".

Opening a door positioned directly beneath the lake, accessed through an intricate set of tunnels that ran beneath the park, the men entered a world unlike anything Tom had ever seen. All around were men and women participating in an assortment of physical tasks; some familiar to him and some completely foreign. "These are the Go'El."

On one end a woman catapulted her slight frame over multiple obstacles, through tunnels and underneath small surfaces to disengage a weapon from an unidentifiable person. It appeared that all of the interactive obstacles and people were tangible holograms. But it wasn't the paraphernalia around the woman or even the person she was fighting that were prominent in this picture, as much as the actions which she was accomplishing. Her body twisted in ways that Tom wished he could replicate but could not imagine himself being able to perform. Not only was she able to constrict her body in what appeared to be complete disregard for her skeleton, but she showed shear strength in holding her body in a plank-like position. Then she would pull her arms into a constant state of ninety degree flexing and crawl to her destination. It was astounding. Tom closed his mouth in realization that he was gawking. He turned to take in the other sights.

Another man, about his body age, wielded a laser-like staff. His arms and legs spun almost independently in what appeared to be a perfectly choreographed movement. The staff led one way, then the other, deflecting small shots fired by an opponent. The man's feet circled and pivoted in patterns reminiscent of an ancient dance, and it all seemed perfectly natural.

Tom's eyes turned again to find a simple climbing wall. Two women were almost floating from one step to the next, racing to ring a bell at the top. Instead, however, of doing what Tom expected and climbing back down, the two women consecutively rang the bell. Then they unceremoniously pushed away from the wall, which stood about four stories from the floor, and jumped, and landing like cats, they scampered away to a new trial. It was only then that Tom realized there had been no harnesses or spotters.

"It looks other-worldly, I know. Just remember, nothing is more sacred than the secret of our existence, so you must suppress some of your abilities in order to protect yourself and the Go'El. Displays like that," he gestured to the jumping women, "cannot happen in the Athoos world...unless absolutely necessary."

In another holographic demonstration, two men closer to Andreas's body age were authenticating the limits of their strength to a group of trainees. It occurred to Tom that the range in what looked to be the physical age of the Go'El encompassed only a matter of a few years. Tom represented the younger end, while Andreas, the elder. Visually, they didn't look to be more than ten years apart in age. The holographic images he saw appeared to include victims in need of help. One victim was trapped inside a car at a busy intersection. A timer on the wall indicated that within eight seconds the trainee was able to peal apart the metal of the mangled car with one hand, and with the other arm lift the two hundred pound victim from the wreckage. The group of trainees cheered as Tom scrutinized each action with envy. His palms itched to push his new body to its limits. Saving the woman on the train tracks, just a vague memory now, had been only the beginning.

Andreas said, "Remember, we're not indestructible. For example, I wouldn't recommend taking a bullet, although it wouldn't affect you the way it would have in your other life."

"What do you mean? Can I die? And what happens then?"

Andreas walked through the gym as he spoke. "You have already died, Tom. Think of this as a rebirth. You've been given a second chance to make a difference, and you now have the capability to do it."

"How far have you tested your limits?"

Andreas thought for a moment. Multiple examples raced through his mind, but one in particular stood out. "I wasn't on duty. There were no lives to save. I was simply going on vacation with an Athoos friend I'd made soon after I came here, probably filling a need to bridge the gap between lives. He didn't know who I had been or what I had become, or what I was capable of doing, but he was the first non-Go'El friend I had made after my transition. And the last...

"We boarded the plane, chatting about the hike we'd be making in the canyon. I had never been and it was something I had always wanted to see, but I had just never made it there. The Go'El are encouraged to rest when we can and to experience things that we weren't able to experience during our lifetime. It's difficult not to become worn down through what we see and experience as Go'El, and refocusing becomes easier when we can stop and acknowledge the true beauty of this world.

"Anyway, I was reading a book when the plane took off. Maybe I should have looked out the window, or maybe I should have been listening more closely, I don't know. I never saw it coming, and I've tasted the bitterness of blame since that day. People from the ground said the plane burst into a fireball not long after takeoff." Andreas's tortured look emoted shivers from Tom. "Our skin will burn, but it will heal just as fast. Even the cells in our throats will revive as quickly as smoke depletes them. That's what killed the others. I pounded out the emergency door and had four children in my arms when I jumped. But when I got them to the ground, they were already gone." Andreas looked up at Tom as he spoke, but Tom knew he was seeing something else altogether. "I had to leave them in the wreckage."

"Why?"

"I knew that I couldn't be found standing at the site of a plane crash and claim that I was the only survivor. Some of the Go'El have done that in the past, but I just couldn't do it. He was my friend, and I watched him burn as my body healed. So I just disappeared. Since then, it's been...difficult...to make friends with anyone who doesn't know about me, who I am, what I am... It also made me understand that while dying on the other side was hard on me, it was intolerable for those I left behind." Andreas turned back to Tom, "Nothing can prepare you for that."

Pushing through the farthest door in the vast space, Tom's eyes moved to a room full of recruits with what looked like sunglasses on their faces. "What are they doing?" he asked quietly.

"They are in simulations; don't worry, you can talk as loudly as you want. The sims are visually loaded through their glasses, but also connected to the brainstem in order to create a prevarication of emotion." Andreas gestured to the glasses-clad individuals. "Nothing can prepare you for the emotional turmoil that comes with your new life. These simulators can provide you with a virtual reality that evokes emotions that you have never felt before."

The last room Andreas took Tom through was an intelligence training simulation. As they entered the room, Tom walked through a haze of numbers and equations seemingly floating through the air. Trainees simply used their fingers to write on the holographic screens containing the mathematical systems. In other parts of the room men and women sat in groups of three or four wearing the sunglasses similar to those in the previous room.

"They are in a simulation, together. That way they are able to solve problems collectively." Tapping his head with a finger, he continued, "Two heads are better than one, and all that." Andreas's mask of joviality seemed to slip whenever training exercises were taking place.

"How long will I train?" Tom asked without taking his eyes off the activities of the others in the room.

"Until you're ready."

"How will I know I'm ready?"

"You'll know," said Andreas definitively.

CHAPTER FOURTEEN

"*D*ammit! She bit me! I can't believe she bit me!" Rubbing her arm over the perfect indentations of what were still Clara's original gleaming teeth, Elaina moved away from her grandmother as if she was being preyed upon.

"You're not my granddaughter!" Clara announced to the entire facility to which she had recently been moved. She had broken her hip just days before.

Had Elaina's mother not been there, she never would have believed that her γιαγιά had been taken down by a swan. Seriously, a swan had attacked her grandmother. Clara and her daughter, Elaina's mother, had been peacefully walking the track just days before near her home where the swan had clearly been nesting. Regardless, Clara had barely made a motion. "Aren't those swans gorgeous?" she'd said, gently gesturing in their direction; and whether the swan was simply pissed off that day, or whether it had grown tired of the incessant statement that had come from Clara's lips, they would never know.

But that day, the swan had had enough.

Elongating its "gorgeous" wings, it rose to almost the

61

height of the two women and aggressively beat its wings. Thankfully, Elaina's mother had been holding Γιαγιά's arm and prevented her from falling head first onto the pavement. However, the crack of her hip could not be prevented, and that crack is what had landed Clara in an institution for rehabilitation that was beginning to register as the beginning of the end.

Upon entering the facility, post-surgery, Clara began to shed any semblance of the light she once represented. Instead of moments of cloudiness infiltrating the brightness, it seemed the other way around. Her acrimony increased exponentially and was no longer solely fixated on a few 'lucky' family members. She would yell at the staff, scream at the other patients, and yet occasionally revert to empathy for those around her. It was a Greek chorus of deep resonating tones, sporadically dispersed by melodic insults; an overture to a life no longer hers.

Who was this person who had been forced into restraints?

Now, in her anger, she had lashed out at Elaina, biting her right forearm.

Elpis swiveled his chair in a room that Clara had entered more than once. Today, he looked somehow different. He wasn't dressed in his usual robes; he seemed casual, but not necessarily comfortable. His lightly-colored khakis snaked down his long legs, and his pale green button-down shirt was tucked neatly into his waistband. His eyes seemed clouded by stress. It was as if he wore many lifetimes on his face. For the first time she wondered just how long he had played this role.

"There is no lesson today," Elpis announced without looking up. And like a rambling old man he continued almost to himself: "Technically, there are lessons in everything, but I will not teach you a lesson today. I am simply asking that you begin practicing your 'medicine', as it were."

Clara had never heard Elpis speak so disjointedly. His focus appeared to be elsewhere. "What do you mean? What's going on?"

"It's time for your first incursion into the mind of the Poneros, not as my protégé, but as my advisor. I've sent two in already and they are going to need our help. Here's what we know in this moment." Elpis brushed the tablet in front of him in a swift upward motion, sweeping information onto the overhead screens.

Although Clara had no memory of her former life, it nevertheless seemed strange that she was able to use technology with such ease. Absentmindedly rubbing her fingers over the keys in front of her, she took in the information presented to her at an impressive speed.

Clara's lips moved slightly, more out of habit than necessity. "I am not sure that I understand enough about the politics," she said aloud to Elpis.

"The authorities won't step in because they are using him for something bigger. Still, he bought the guns and has been buying ammunition for weeks. He's a psychiatric analyst for the military. There's something about the circle of circumstances surrounding him that makes me feel uneasy. I think he might attack his own. We can't let that happen." Elpis hung on to those last words like a lifeboat.

Clara turned back to her screen to try to get a better understanding of this man's motivation. If Elpis was right, and she'd had enough conversations with him to know that he rarely said anything without conviction, then this soldier was on the precipice of massacring his peers.

Clara had been told in no uncertain terms that her presence here was a recent decision, albeit fifteen years in the making. All she knew of her other life was that she had suffered from severe Dementia with Alzheimer's riding a close second in the race toward oblivion.

"It is an extremely indolent process. The mind cannot take rapid deterioration; otherwise the soul is rendered useless. As slowly as we pull you apart, we begin to fill the void as well. However, it isn't until full assimilation—where we are now—that you begin to separate the two."

Elpis had allowed her to understand that decisions had been made to evolve their recruitment process, so that no longer was the Go'El the only entity working toward balance.

"Before now, you were simply a vessel of information under construction. Now you are an asset."

Clara focused on reducing her task at hand to an equation of assumptions: 1) If the Go'El has evolved from recruiting only operatives to cultivating a true brain trust, then the likelihood of the Poneros doing something similar is quite high; 2) Elpis has discussed the need for balance, which is in a constant state of turmoil; therefore, the Poneros may attempt to unbalance the mind, if that is not already their objective; 3) Our history suggests that the Poneros optimize the emotional weaknesses and insecurities of the human population, so why would they change that strategy now?

Her mind cycled endlessly through information: she would take it in, categorize it, and then isolate it until it was needed. It was as if her mind could divide itself when necessary to address various problems, and as her assimilation progressed, she was even able to tap into elements of her genealogical history for information and resources. She found that she could access the hippocampus, essential for memory function, and although she retained no memories of her own life, she was able to access functional memories of what she could only assume were those of her family members throughout history. For example, if there had been a lawyer in her family, she had no need to learn information about law; she'd simply gained access to it through shared cellular memory.

Clara had read an article refuting the urban myth stating that humans only used ten percent of their brains. If that were the case, then creating a new and improved

Clara would have been accomplished simply by increasing the percentage of brain activity. However, studies had found through brain imaging that even Athoos at rest used all parts of the brain, albeit at a low level. Likewise, it followed that some types of brain damage should not have any effect on people if they only used a small percentage of brain capacity, however that was not what the study had revealed.

Clara was now able to use her mind in a way that no Athoos could. She could dissect multiple levels of problems in order to find divergent solutions, rather than being limited by a single assumption. With this, the speed by which she could process information and export it had increased exponentially.

She could also alter her physical being by manipulating her own DNA. Each person's genetic code has dominant traits and recessive ones. These are seen when one parent has brown eyes, while the other has blue. A child from those parents will receive both colors from their parents, but one will lie in the background, while the other color is dominant. Clara could now access both colors, changing her eyes to any color within her genetic code.

"What was it that you told me about the easiest way to divide the population? Gender wars, right? Split us in half. What are some other examples of that? Can we look for some kind of pattern?" Clara typed furiously on the computer in front of her trying to gather information as quickly as possible.

While typing, she glanced at the monitor to the left of Elpis's arm. Andreas and Tom were en route to a conversation with the ammo-buying military psychologist, and whether he killed today or tomorrow, the shrapnel would penetrate.

CHAPTER FIFTEEN

"So this guy is a practicing Muslim psychiatrist who told his also practicing Muslim psychiatrist friend, that he should not join the American military because Muslims shouldn't kill other Muslims?" Tom looked at his mentor for answers as they neared the compound.

"Well, yeah, but this isn't a Muslim thing. This is a crazy thing," Andreas responded with a cool head, but ever-ready eyes.

"Believe me, I agree. I'm just trying to get it straight." Again, Tom was simply running through the list of facts and trying to decipher between political responses and what was necessary to proceed in a conversation with the subject.

"Unfortunately, too many people overlook the fact that being Muslim doesn't make you a terrorist, just as being German never made anyone a Nazi." Andreas kicked up dust from the rocks underneath his feet. Even after so many years, he still marveled at his ability to see the particles as they settled once again. In his old life he had worn glasses, but he didn't need them here. Every now and then he found himself readjusting the imaginary frames, pushing his fingers to his temples and finding only skin. It was a habit that wouldn't quite leave him, but was comforting just the same.

"Once, when he was presenting what was supposedly a medical lecture to other psychiatrists, he started talking about Islam. There's a time and a place for religion, I guess. I imagine for soldiers it would be hard to deal with what they see and not hope for something bigger than themselves to be pulling the strings. But he tells this group of psychiatrists that the Qur'an teaches that anyone who doesn't believe in Islam will be sent to hell, decapitated, set on fire and have burning oil poured down his throat."

"Sounds like the kind of guy that really brings people together. I'm sure the mosques are dying to recruit him."

"The Associated Press added that his little fireside chat included justifications for suicide bombings, too. Now, I'm no expert on the Qur'an, yet..."

They both listened through their ear implants as updates regarding the suspect were delivered. In fact, there was so much information being transmitted that each was listening to a separate broadcast in order to optimize information.

Andreas spoke first: "He sold his furniture two days ago. I'm betting we have less time than we thought."

CHAPTER SIXTEEN

*"D*ivisive decisions in our history: segregation, slavery, racism, homophobia..." Clara was thinking aloud now and at breakneck speed. Elpis was awed by the speed at which she was taking in information and releasing it for his feedback.

"What do religious texts say about racism?" He was now using her as a reference guide. Her stays with him were lasting longer and he enjoyed the company.

"Well, the whole concept of racism was Athoos-born. Probably Poneros planted. There is just as much in the Bible that denounces that kind of ugliness as there are interpretative stories that condone human disassociation. Any imbecile can decide that because Eve came after Adam, it must mean that women are inferior."

He adored her sense of humor and was amazed by its presence even without memories to induce it. "You should make the claim that he made a trial run with Adam, a rough draft, but he acquired perfection with Eve."

"I'll get right on that...after we prevent another mass murder." Elpis humored her.

"Anyway, Galatians says, 'There is neither Jew nor

Greek, there is neither slave nor free, there is no male and female, for you are all one in Christ Jesus.' John taught 'that you love one another; just as I have loved you, you also are to love one another.' The golden rule is everywhere. Where do you think it stemmed from?" Clara's cheeks pinked as her frustration toward intolerance grew.

"So, what do we have here? The Bible and the Talmud are aligned with the ideals of equality. What about the Qur'an? Muhammad has been criticized for centuries because he had followers put his teachings onto scrolls, since he was able to neither read nor write. Many of the Go'El believed that at least one of those followers was Poneros. Sometimes writing with ambiguity allows just as much dark as light. The same goes for the Bible. I am sure you have heard theories that there are missing scrolls; writings that never made it into the final draft. People have put so much stock in these writings, rather than in their hearts. That is where God resides, not within the black ink on a page." Elpis shook his head in resignation. "But, where will the Poneros hit now? He claims to be Muslim. He is American military. He is a psychologist. He is a man."

"The Qur'an says, 'and mankind is naught but a single nation.' The Prophet Muhammed taught that 'All men are equal in Islam, the Arab has no superiority over the non-Arab, nor does the non-Arab have superiority over the Arab, save in the fear of God.' He respected Jesus and his teachings. There was no conflict there because God really did send these Prophets as vessels for his teachings!" Looking up in an attempt to settle her anxiety, she ran her hand through her hair, stopping to rake her nails across her scalp. It was comforting, and she wondered briefly if it stemmed from a human experience. Just as quickly, she returned to her original thought. "Of course there was more than one prophet. There are a lot a people on this planet. Why is it so abhorrent to assume that there are many prophets teaching the same lessons of God in different ways to diverse groups of people? That seems logical to me."

"Hence the reason why you are here..."

"But, Elpis, I don't know who this man is targeting. I don't think he will go after women. I really don't see any reason that he will target those of other races, or even other religious affiliations. It doesn't sound like class warfare, or even political vitriol. But he conveys the impression that he is disillusioned with his job." Clara's head shot up quickly, and so did she. "He's going to target his work place. He's going to execute members of the military!"

CHAPTER SEVENTEEN

*T*he first shot rang out as Andreas and Tom were passing their credentials through the initial checkpoint, and it was ironic that their identities were being scrutinized by security just as the worst kind of breach was happening from within.

"Hurry!"

"We have no idea where he is."

"Use your senses. You can calculate how far away the shot was by the regressions of sound as it echoes toward us. Can you smell the powder? Track it all!" Andreas filtered the physical information with which they were inundated.

The checkpoint gate stood about thirty feet high with a bird's nest presiding over the post. Another office beneath housed four to five military personnel, all of whom transformed from secretaries into soldiers within seconds as the shots rang out. The sniper in the nest, Tom noted, was not unsteady in his reaction, but lowered himself as Tom had, in order to determine the origin. As Tom and Andreas ran toward a still unidentified destination, Tom kept watch on the sniper, hoping that his bird's eye view would point them in the right direction.

Tom and Andreas decided to split up in order to cover more ground. It seemed the logical thing to do. Each building was simple and fundamental, like barns for human warriors. Tom peeked inside each entrance as he passed, measuring the need to enter.

More shots were fired.

The sounds bounced from building to building, and both Tom and Andreas stopped long enough to redirect. Like animals in a forest, they craned their necks to detect smells, sounds and movements. Another single shot fired. They were closer, but not close enough.

"He's in the processing center!" Clara's voice rang through both of their earpieces. "The building is two hundred meters southwest of where you are standing."

Both men went into full sprint. Like gazelles, they appeared to others as if floating in between steps. Amidst the chaos that had churned throughout the post, few noticed these two oddities making their way to the center of it.

They both halted, and then peeked through windows to determine their next course of action. What they saw was unnerving. With civilians and military operatives interspersed throughout the center, it was difficult to determine who the targets were.

But it was not difficult to see the blood.

Tom and Andreas were at the far end of the building, about one hundred meters from where their suspect stood. They spotted him because one soldier had bravely decided to rush toward him, only to be met with a bullet. He dropped abruptly to the ground. Tom and Andreas crept under the guise of the pandemonium. Staying close to book cases that lined the back wall, they insinuated their way into the target's vicinity.

Just as they attempted to communicate with one another, a second soldier lifted a folding table and threw it in the shooter's direction. Hardly fazed, the culprit took aim and shot the soldier's left hip. With a gasp, the soldier dropped to the floor and then crawled to the nearest safe haven, a cubicle near the corner.

Tom's first reaction was to go for the living victim, but Andreas seized his arm tightly. *Stay focused.* Tom argued with his heart. *Stay with the original target. Minimize casualties.* He nodded, more to himself than in response to Andreas.

They dropped to the ground as they no longer had the shelves as camouflage. Creeping behind various office objects, they propelled themselves toward the target. Surprisingly agile on their stomachs, they swam through the carpeting from one side to the other.

Andreas took a moment to look over a fallen file cabinet. Just as they both stopped, their breathing ceased as they saw the target sweep the dot of his pistol over the heads of five civilians hidden beneath desks. Then, just as rapidly as he had aimed, he lifted the scope and walked through the nearest door into the open air. Tears surged down one of the civilian's cheeks. Her chestnut hair damp with expressed emotion, she leaned heavily on her hands and whimpered.

"Clara's right. He is only attacking soldiers, not civilians," Andreas whispered as they rushed to the other side of the center.

"It is military policy that soldiers are not allowed to carry personal weapons," Tom responded to the unasked question as to why no one had confronted the shooter.

More shots fired outside, forcing Tom and Andreas to make the decision to leave the wounded behind. Before passing through the threshold of the door, Andreas removed his leather belt and tossed it to a nearby civilian hiding behind a desk. "Secure the door behind us with this. They will take care of you." He pointed to the medical team that was now rushing in through the far doors. Taking a quick look outside, Tom gestured for Andreas to follow, one on the far side, the other slinking against the wall on the near side of the next building. They had lost sight of the target, but found a woman at the door of her military police vehicle, slumped toward the rear tire. Tom rushed over, feeling for a pulse in the unconscious woman's neck. "Looks like the one on her hand is shrapnel; bleeding appears to be controlled. She's got a bullet in her knee and a second one has shattered her femur. Medic!" he called. He knew that yelling was not the best course of action, but this woman was dying. He pressed his hands securely around her leg and pulled a sweatshirt from the seat of her car. Quickly, he tied a tourniquet and positioned it over the wound. A medic was running their way.

Andreas's movements mirrored those of the shooter. Jogging, he stayed close to the nearest building. Without warning, Andreas's shoulder was brushed by a soldier emerging from the building. Since he had turned quickly to look at the victim, his reaction was to snap his head back into a fighter's stance, now seeing the stream of soldiers running in their direction. Like rats fleeing fire, they couldn't get away from the rain of gunshots that were cracking around them. Bodies were falling as Tom and Andreas looped around the other side of the building rather than fight against the stream of men and women looking for cover.

"Put your weapon down—now!"

If Tom had chosen a weapon of more fire power and less margin for error, he would have succeeded in taking out the target with a low probability of self-harm. However, the fourteen onlookers, and possibly those fleeing soldiers, would have had visual proof of the existence of a power far beyond that of the American military. And Tom and Andreas were going to have a hard enough time explaining their presence here as it was.

"Drop your weapon, sir!" Tom repeated his command, adding a 'sir', which appealed to Andreas. But the target did not heed the warning. He spun quickly, and Tom hesitated for a fraction of a second in hope that the target would turn rather than attack.

He was wrong.

In that second of hesitation, Tom noticed two things: first, the gunman touched his ear; and second, a billowing mass of a dress draped and disappeared around the side of the nearest building. Was the shooter wired for communication? Just then, a bullet struck wide, ricocheting off the gutter behind them. Tom and Andreas shot simultaneously. The shells skimmed past one another and entered the shooter's body. The target dropped his weapon.

But not before he had pinched his trigger one last time.

CHAPTER EIGHTEEN

"Get out of here! You are not my granddaughter!" Clara's lightning strike of an outburst was severe and sudden.

Elaina cringed at the hurtful words, but pulled on the armor that she had learned to wear in moments like this one. "Γιαγιά, I *am* your granddaughter and nothing will change that." She was tired. Layered onto her normal life, she had to deal with this abuse. Elaina had been making attempts to stop by Clara's home as often as she could in order to give her mother and aunt some reprieve. But after days of teaching, and before coming home to her own two little ones, she was worn down. Shoulders slumping, she leaned back in her chair, anticipating the abuse that was sure to come. Some days she couldn't help but question an existence like this.

"Γιαγιά, I need to go home. I have to pick up the kids."

"What kids? You *are* a kid. Have you been sleeping around again?"

"Γιαγιά, I'm married. I have two kids." Elaina rolled her eyes. Why did she even try?

"Two kids you never bring to see me. I'm all alone here. Take me home. Don't you love me?"

Those words pierced Elaina's soul more deeply than any vulgarity that Clara might expel. She looked at her grandmother and forced herself to remember the person that she had been.

It had been ten years since Clara had volunteered to help Elaina set up her first classroom, and they had spent hours together on that late summer day stacking book shelves. They had talked, laughed and dreamed together. They'd listened to music, and Clara never ceased to amaze Elaina with her ability to embrace modern culture while remaining true to her Greek traditions. Who else could shake her booty to Rhianna in her eighties?

And they had made it an annual tradition. Γιαγιά would meet Elaina each year to help her set up her room. Until one year, Γιαγιά hadn't shown up. Elaina had first worried and then called repeatedly until she finally reached her grandmother. "I got lost," Clara confessed, her voice smaller than Elaina could ever remember it sounding.

Now she was no longer the mentor she had once been to Elaina; she was more like the child to Elaina's adult.

"I will bring the kids tomorrow." She swept her hand through Clara's unkempt hair and pulled her covers up a little higher. Clara stared directly into Elaina's eyes, as if the real Clara was fighting her way through the jungle of confusion.

"I love you, κούκλα."

Clara hadn't called Elaina 'her doll' in years, and with those two syllables, Elaina felt tears prick the sides of her eyes. She squeezed her grandmother one last time, fighting the onslaught of emotion, and walked through the door.

Clara would not see tomorrow.

CHAPTER NINETEEN

"*S*o this is what this feels like." Tom blew out desperately trying to purge his body of the pain.

"Where did he get you?" Andreas felt his heart limp behind him in response as he turned to see his new partner with blood now seeping beneath his gray shirt. Desperately, he ran to Tom's side and lifted his shirt, gently peeling it away from the sticky substance. Sticky is good, he assessed. Sticky means his body is trying to coagulate the blood. But, where is the bullet? Where is the wound? There is so much blood...

Tom tipped his head back, remaining remarkably calm considering the truth of the situation. His memories of hospital visits and the slow torture of chemotherapy kept him solidly rooted in this reality. In comparison, a bullet wound felt like a paper cut. Andreas desperately wiped the blood away with his own shirt, which he had hastily removed. He couldn't keep up with the flood of crimson flowing from Tom's eerily still body.

On their other side, the full power of the military had descended on the shooter, who had dropped where he had been targeted.

Finally, Andreas found the wound, realizing that the bullet was still lodged in Tom's stomach. Rather than allow shrapnel from the shell to enter Tom's bloodstream, he was going to need to remove it. "Tom, I have to take it out. And it won't tickle."

"What do you have to take out? What's inside me?"

"The bullet is still remarkably intact, probably due to the impermeability of your skin. But there are three pieces of shrapnel that I need to take out along with it. If I don't, your body will heal too quickly and absorb them into your bloodstream. They will kill you."

"Do it," Tom spit out. "Take it out." His fingers flexed in the dirt beneath him, as if holding an invisible hand.

"Are you sure? I don't have anything to use except my fingers. This is really going to hurt."

"I had cancer. Can it hurt worse than that?"

"We can try," Andreas responded in a light tone that didn't reflect his dire mood. He had to get in quickly and get out. He was less worried about infection, which he knew Tom's body could fight off, but he was very concerned about his ability to keep from pushing anything deeper into the major artery which ran about a half inch from the exposed site. That would kill him instantly. Andreas looked at his fingers first, trying to determine the size of his natural forceps and how wide he would have to open them to gain access and remove the fragments.

This was not going to be easy.

"How can I help?"

Both men snapped to attention at the familiar voice that no longer resided in their earpieces.

"Clara? Where did you come from?"

The light reflected off her hair. Clara's eyes had a clarity to them unlike anything Andreas had ever seen. Her skin was remarkably smooth considering what he knew of her age. She looked strong but feminine. He looked from his bloodied young friend to Clara and simply wanted to protect her from the reality before her.

"I'm not really able to answer those kinds of questions, it seems. However, I have become an expert in medical procedures. Apparently, someone down my genealogical line was a doctor." Tapping on her head she continued, "It looks like I've got all that information right here." Rubbing her hands together, she looked at her patient. "Tom, I may need to put my fingers inside your belly."

With her purpose deeply engrained, she experienced a filter, almost as if a new lens had been placed over her eye, allowing her to see an object with the power of an x-ray. All images contain wavelengths of light. The length is longer or shorter depending on the kind of image. Visible light, what a normal human can see, has longer wavelengths than x-ray light. Clara could control her parietal lobe in such a way that allowed her to see both. With this new skill, she scanned his body for potential wounds.

"He's got a bullet in his gut and we have to take it out. It may be ill-positioned." Andreas tried to explain to Clara the desperateness of the situation without alarming Tom more than necessary.

"I see." Clara calmly collected all the information presented to her and visually assessed the same predicament to which Andreas had alluded. "Visible light has a particular amplitude and frequency depending on the image. If I could just..." She smiled in triumph.

"Amplitude?" Andreas pressed.

"Every image of light is made up of waves that go up and down to certain heights. That height is called amplitude. If I can filter what image my brain sees by affecting the amplitude, then I can see images like an x-ray machine or MRI. My fingers are smaller, and I have nails. I'll do it." She'd made her claim and had provided evidence. "It looks as though there are three fragments besides the bullet itself. The wet sound faintly heard from the wound indicates that Tom's lung may be at risk." In her mind, there was no arguing with logic. And Andreas was not about to argue with her either.

"Are you ready, Tom?" Clara was able to balance every problematic detail with every necessary response. She calmed her body by focusing on the steps. Counting them off in her head, she charged the line and waited for the go ahead.

"I think so." Tom's eyes widened as her pincers poised at the wound's entrance. There was no way to prepare for this.

"One, two..."

His groan of agony echoed through the base as if he were a wounded animal, forcing the other military personnel to turn toward the sound. Even though Tom and Andreas had taken down the shooter, it was almost as if no one really saw them or regarded them as important.

"What happened to three?" Tom seethed.

"You know things only hurt more when you anticipate them. I spared you."

"That was sparing me?"

"I'm not done."

Tom bit down on his lip as the pain resurfaced. He had taught himself long ago not to outwardly show suffering. He thought it had helped his mother to not know every horrid experience he'd had. Those skills served him well now, because the Athoos seemed too distracted with other victims and with identifying the shooter to notice what was happening only feet away from them.

"All done. Not too bad, right?" Clara smiled triumphantly, holding three pieces of shell and the rest of the bullet. "Do you want to keep these?" she asked Tom as she rose to her feet and gently helped him to sit up.

As soon as the bullets and fragments had been removed, the openings they had created in Tom's body began to close, and his superior flesh did what it was made to do.

He healed.

CHAPTER TWENTY

*T*hese are for the living, not the deceased.

If my grandmother had a say in this, she would have us all play cards, watch classic movies and dance until the sun came up because that's who she was.

She was never this stiff-suited, unsmiling, quiet diva that became her life.

She was music; both classical and jazz.

She was sarcasm; witty, never biting.

She was beauty; external and internal.

She was.

She was the kind of woman who had cocktail napkins that said $%&# Birthdays.

She was the kind of woman who never needed to drink to have fun, save the occasional bubbles over champagne.

She was the kind of woman who would join the game of using toothpicks to pick lifesavers off the floor without using her hands.

She was the kind of woman who had dinner parties for her granddaughter's high school friends.

She was.

I still can't get used to those words, even though she

became a past tense an awfully long time ago.

But, Γιαγιά, even if you can't remember, I'll remember for you.

I love you. And there is no "was" about that.

I'll see you again...

Eulogies were for the living, Elaina thought to herself. She wasn't sure if she could go through with reading this in church, in front of all of Γιαγιά's family and friends. But she had to. Γιαγιά had always been about presentation. And this was the ultimate.

I just can't believe that she's gone. Elaina thought to herself as she wrote in the quiet confines of Clara's now empty apartment. Boxes of emptied drawers and stacks of photographs in a montage of frames scattered the surfaces of this memory receptacle. *I wanted this*, she reminded herself over and over as the tears continued to flow. *I wanted her to have peace.* She held an icon that had once watched over her grandmother's bedside table. *That's what this is all about, right? We do our best here, we suffer some, we find joy, we help others...and then we have peace.*

Elaina closed her journal, took one last look around her childhood, and shut the door behind her.

CHAPTER TWENTY-ONE

"You're all right, then?" Elpis asked after the trio had returned. His eyes darted around the bloodstained shirts that covered both Tom's and Andreas' bodies.

Tom lifted his shirt for proof. "It's still a little red, but Clara had her fingers inside four bullet holes in my body less than an hour ago. And now it's just a little red." He looked from his torso to Elpis in utter amazement. He couldn't stop smiling.

"But you have to be careful not to take this for granted," said Andreas. "You felt the pain, so you know you aren't exempt from human vulnerability. Let that pain be a reminder that you are not invincible."

"First day on the job and I saved your behinds." Clara went as far as to pat her own back. "Don't want to toot my own horn, but...toot, toot."

All three men laughed and seated themselves in a debriefing room beneath the grounds of Yellowstone. It was a room that Tom and Clara had never entered, being that this was the first mission from which they needed to debrief. Clara rested her hand over the dimpled leather and felt the soft, yet firm give of a chair she wasn't quite sure was real or hologram. She was still getting used to this place, so different from anything she could comprehend. She had no memories of the other life, but she intuited the realities and variances of the two locations.

And now she was here to stay.

"How did you know that you had...that you were permanent?" Elpis looked at Clara. She would never get used to his responding questions that consistently seemed to peel back the layers of her thoughts. Not remembering was intensely unnerving. And it appeared that Elpis was most understanding of that fact. He gently probed for his own understanding, but Clara could tell that he sought to comfort her as well.

Now, Tom and Andreas turned toward her, and she felt herself readjust her position in the chair that felt unnaturally warm in that moment. Tom still looked at her like she was a shiny new object that he simply wanted to discover and collect. Andreas, on the other hand, looked at her very differently. The physicality of Clara had altered only slightly from who she was on the other side. Of course, her age change had been drastic, since she now resided in the body of her thirty- something former self. Elpis had explained that this had *happened*, yet it was information she was forced to trust rather than understand. And that trust was not coming easily, she had found.

She didn't have any special strength or healing ability like the Go'El, but her mind now seemed to function at a speed that far surpassed what she sensed to be normal. And it seemed she was only touching the surface of her capabilities by tapping into this unique vision. Not only that, but she was able to manipulate her genetic makeup by pulling to the surface that which had previously lain dormant. Today she felt like a doctor. She had treated gunshot wounds without hesitating. She'd realized that along with her ability to garner new information, she could also follow some sort of evolutionary path into the past.

Not only could she imprint information in her mind of which she'd only briefly glimpsed, but she could solve multidimensional problems at a speed with which anyone else adds an item to a grocery list. She had been sent here for her intelligence. Elpis had flat out told her so. She had struggled with that; her initial thoughts had fallen on those faceless individuals that she had left behind. Although she couldn't remember, she knew they existed. She had learned enough about Dementia and Alzheimer's to understand its effects not only on the victim, but on those who care for them. She had felt her stomach drop in the moment that Elpis had told her, "You are here to bring us hope again. We have simply been surviving these last years. It has felt not only to us, but to Athoos as well, that the world is a dark place, not worthy of faith. People have turned away from any higher power; they have quieted their prayers and the balance has tipped in favor of the Poneros. We need you. We need you to guide us back to the light."

"What if I can't?" The question had hung between them as she faded back to the other side. She thought if only she could remember her past, maybe it would be the motivation to save a world for which she had no real connection. She felt summoned both an unknown past and an expectant future. And every time she attempted to hold both sides in her mind, a searing pain intensified. She was learning that she needed to let go of her past.

But she had now gained a measure of confidence. She had determined the location of a target and she had arrived just in time to ensure the safety of two Go'El.

"I knew I wasn't on the other side anymore," she said. And in that simple statement there was an undeniable understanding of her own mortality, even if she couldn't remember it. Still, there was a part of her that felt an enormous relief at the loss of whatever life to which she had been clinging. With that relief, she couldn't deny that the pain was subsiding now, which seemed ironic since she couldn't remember to whom or to what she had been tethered. But she felt free here. And she was beginning to feel a sense of belonging to this group of misfits who had started to fill her mind with promise.

"Elpis, I would like to help Clara acclimate to her new surroundings, if she'll have me." Andreas looked to her for a response.

Her attention moved to the speaker. It wasn't his blue eyes, almost crystalline, or his dark, curly hair that made him handsome. It was his confidence. He looked at her like she was the only person in the room.

Elpis gave him a knowing smile that was lost on everyone else, and then continued. "Clara, you will feel tempted to find out more about your old life, but we can't be sure how you might react to those kinds of memories. We have taken steps to ensure that they must remain where they are."

Clara nodded.

"Clara, I would be honored to be your tour guide." Andreas offered her his arm, which was a welcome distraction from the weight of Elpis's words.

"I'm still not quite sure what is to my liking, but I can't think of any reason to resist." Clara's body felt unreasonably light as she jumped to her feet and took Andreas's arm.

CHAPTER TWENTY-TWO

"*W*hat was that about?" Tom asked as he watched the backs of Andreas and Clara dance away.

"Nothing but a memory, I guess," Elpis said as he spun back to his desk.

Tom shook his head, not wanting to delve any further into something he clearly didn't understand. "Do you need me for anything? I should probably change out of these clothes."

Raising a device to Tom's body, Elpis scanned his bones, muscles and ligaments for any signs of distress. "No, rest now." Elpis flipped through multiple screens in front of him. "We'll get back to work tomorrow."

"I'll see you then," Tom returned and headed toward the door.

"Yes, you will." Elpis looked uneasy as Tom retreated.

"So, I hear you rocked it today," Banko said as she picked up her feet and casually rested them on a wooden coffee table in Tom's room.

He leaned back against his plush gray couch and placed his heels on the same table. He'd showered and changed his shirt, but the smell of gun smoke and blood still seemed to linger. He tried to focus on the fact that the day had been perceived a success, and they definitely had saved countless lives, but thirteen people had died before Tom could save them. Thirty more were still in the hospital, while Tom went on with his day in the comfort of his new home. It didn't seem right.

Throughout his training they had been taught about the difficulties of their missions. Happy endings were not guaranteed. Missions were rarely clean. The reality of the conflict that existed between good and evil, Go'El and Poneros, was that there was no winner. Unfortunately, it was the annihilation that Athoos found fascinating. The news was saturated with it. A person could wake up in the morning and read the paper or watch the news and be inundated with one horrific event after another. In turn, people were led to believe that they lived in a world of only pain and suffering. It was far too easy to lose focus on the beauty that existed. Through training, the Go'El were taught to refocus on that beauty in order to counteract the horror.

Lately, he found himself wondering if any Go'El had ever deserted. He wondered what would happen if someone with his powers decided that the Go'El were no longer on the right side of the conflict. Nothing forced him to stay here except the mission—the cause.

Tom missed his mother; he missed his life. Cancer or not, it had felt full. There had been pictures in his room, posters adorning his walls, a life yet to be lived. Here, he felt displaced, not quite here, but no longer there.

"Do you ever miss the other life? Maybe not exactly what it was before you died, but what it could have been if you hadn't?" Tom couldn't look at Banko as he asked the question.

Banko had always seemed comfortable and confident. He wanted to feel like that, too. Sometimes, when he admitted it to himself, he knew it was why he sought her out more than the others. She was the kind of person he hoped he could be. And she was a fantastic friend.

"Where did that come from? Didn't today take away some of that heartache?" She already knew his feelings; she just wanted him to voice them.

"Yeah, I made a difference. I took the shot, and I wasn't sure I had it in me until I watched the guy mowing down innocent people. And then it was like it all just clicked: our training; my death. It all made sense. But why do I still miss my old life?"

Banko shrugged.

"Banko, before I shot him, I think I saw, I mean...I don't know. I'm not sure what I saw."

Banko waited for a moment, searching his eyes for something more, but decided he would tell her more when it felt right to him.

"Did anyone ever tell you that you were an old soul?" Banko picked up some papers that lay on the desk in the corner of the room. Fanning them out, Tom knew she couldn't help but search for answers, even with none apparent.

"What do you mean?"

"You know. Did your mom ever say, 'Tommy, you have an old soul'? Or did you meet someone, and within minutes they would comment, 'Wow, Tommy, you seem so much older than your years'?" Banko turned to him leaning her hip on the now messier desk.

"Yeah, I guess. My mom used to say it a lot, and doctors always made those comments to me, too." Tommy looked to her for a response. "Did you?"

"You talk to most Go'El and they will tell you a similar story. We are all old souls. And with that comes a more acute understanding of what was lost when we died on the other side. I think now that they are recruiting people who don't remember their former lives; it's difficult not to compare. Which do you think is more difficult? Knowing what you miss or not missing anything at all? I really don't know. I have gone back and forth on the merits of both, but I have come up blank." Banko pushed herself from the desk and briskly stepped toward the door. "Come here," she said without waiting to see if Tom would follow.

Outside, the chilled air wrapped itself around Tom's face as he closed the door behind him and turned to follow his friend. He touched the cool railing while walking to the other end of the platform, one floor above the ground.

He was still getting used to this place. His home, he forced himself to think. Slowly, he was acclimating to this existence. Similar to a college dorm, or so he'd heard the comparison, all the new recruits lived in the same complex of apartments. It existed in isolation, tucked into the remote landscape of the land. There were no Athoos in the vicinity, nor would any find it, he guessed. This was harsh terrain. Even the boldest could not physically commit to this level of isolation. When they had a mission, they were simply 'transported' to the scene. Once the mission was finished, they were repatriated on the campus.

Where the money came from to fund the housing and feed all of the Go'El, he didn't know, but thought often to ask. In his other life, he had constantly worried about money. With medical bills mounting, and less time for his mother to work because she didn't want to leave his side in the hospital, money was always a worry. And even before that, they had barely been able to make ends meet, especially after they had left Tom's father behind. And now, Tom had left his mother behind. And still he worried for her. How long would he worry?

Snapping back to the reality of his present circumstance, Tom traced the numbers on the door of Banko's apartment—one identical to his own—as she held it open for him. However, when he crossed the threshold, he found himself in an environment completely different from his nondescript quarters—one of color and inspiration.

Wordlessly, he wandered around the room, as she had obviously welcomed his exploration. He ran his finger over each picture along the tables and walls, carefully scrutinizing each one. Not only were the tabletops cluttered with moments, but the walls were as well. Peppered with quotes, Tom stopped to read each one.

A lengthier one was first, looking as if Banko had typed it on computer paper and decided to frame it.

It read, "*A clear awareness and correct understanding of the nature of death can enable us to live without fear and with strength, clarity of purpose and joy. Buddhism views the universe as a vast living entity, in which cycles of individual life and death are repeated without end. Death is therefore a necessary part of the life process, making possible renewal and new growth.*"

Tom turned to Banko and studied her face. Her dark eyes were immaculately framed by black straight hair, cut at an angle around her petite face. Although she was small in stature, there was a strength and agility to her every movement that gave her a more powerful appearance. Too caught up in his interpretation of the quote, he refrained from asking hers. Returning to his purpose, he moved on to the next picture on the wall. It was of Banko, another recruit and Tom, arms wrapped around each other on the final day of their training.

"Tom, I know you are probably getting tired of hearing it, but it really is a balance. We lost something there, but we gained something here. We had to live that life to be strong enough to live this one. How many Athoos did you know who fought cancer and took that fight with them? I took it with me. I feel older. I feel stronger and I feel wiser. And I am thankful for that every day. Am I sad because I lost my family, some of my culture and even a little bit of myself? Sure I am. But that doesn't mean that I can't make something of what we have here. Look around you. You already have friends...really, a family. You definitely have a sister," she gestured to herself. "And the rest, you will make for yourself. That is the renewal that

Buddhists embrace. Maybe I'm lucky, and what I believed before I came here prepared me for all of this. Either way, I will make the best of it."

Tom was impressed. During training sessions, her quickness and skills dominated all others. In conversation, her wisdom, compassion and conviction surpassed others. And now, her fierce friendship filled him with everything he needed this day.

CHAPTER TWENTY-THREE

Andreas and Clara walked out of the planning room doors and into the sun. The moment they walked outside, Clara drew in a breath and looked up in the direction of the heat. Closing her eyes, she soaked in the warmth as her lips curled with contentment. This was the first moment in this existence when she'd consciously made a human memory. She wondered if it would remain or be rendered unnecessary later.

Andreas stopped with her and stared at her innocent reaction. The light reflected off her hair and her lashes rested on her olive cheeks, fluttering only slightly under the weight of intense thought. She stilled her face toward the sun, harnessing its power. Andreas couldn't begin to imagine living with superior intelligence but no memory. His memories pushed him forward through the strife that seemed to be his every day calling. His memories had led him to this moment with this woman. And he wouldn't be willing to relinquish them for anything.

Clara slid her arm out from Andreas's and walked toward a grassy opening that lay between buildings in their complex. She slid her shoes from her feet and curled her toes into the cool grass. Her smile grew large as she took in the nuances of nature, as if seeing them for the first time.

"Are you remembering something?" Andreas couldn't help but ask. The sun hid behind clouds for a moment, enveloping him in shadow, while Clara still glowed.

Her eyes turned to focus on her companion and then she paused, thinking about how to answer. He was handsome—strikingly so. It wasn't as if she hadn't noticed, but it was the first time since she'd met him that she was able to truly appreciate it. His eyes had depth of character, of fortune and loss, and love. His hands hung by his sides, but appeared restless, as he waited for her answer.

"The way my mind processes my former life is more creation than recall. I was told that I was sick, that I had a family, so in turn, I have emotionally created a fictional life based on that information. I probably did that to cope with this reality." The last part was more an aside than an explanation to Andreas. "It's almost as if I read about those things in a book. The experiences that seem real to me are in the present. This seems real to me. You seem real. And yet, I seem to be aware of some undefinable difference. My brain somehow comprehends that my body has been altered, biologically and hormonally, by the rays of the sun. I need vitamin D in order to thrive. I know these things, but I don't know how it is possible. I don't understand the context or the mechanism. After what I know of my illness, I guess it feels like heaven." Engulfed by her surroundings, Clara smiled at Andreas almost with resignation.

"I can understand that feeling." He looked right at her, hoping she didn't miss the innuendo. Then he lightened the moment by extending his arm again and asking, "Would you like to stay here and soak in your vitamin D, or walk a bit and see your new digs?"

"My new home?" Clara questioned.

"Well, you didn't expect us to leave you out on the

street, did you?" Andreas pulled her closer as she returned the gesture and linked her arm with his.

"Funny, I hadn't thought about it," Clara said as she pulled her brows together in deep thought.

"It's okay that you don't think of everything, you know." Andreas nudged her gently in jest.

"But isn't that why I'm here?" Clara asked, feeling the weight of her circumstances.

Andreas hadn't thought of that. He hadn't thought of the pressure that she must feel being the first of her kind, recruited for the reasons that she scarcely understood. She didn't have guidance like he had in Elpis or The Professor when he arrived. She didn't have counterparts who could identify with the feelings that she had in determining her place in this world. She must feel so isolated. "I'm sorry," he murmured.

"For what?"

"For not understanding what this must feel like for you."

"Well, isn't that a stereotype of men? Not understanding women's emotions?" she elbowed his ribs gently.

"What book did Elpis give you to learn that? I am going to need to rip some pages out and do some rewriting." He couldn't help but smile at her. The back and forth banter felt refreshing, something he had deeply missed. Where Elpis had been an incredible mentor, and later a friend, something had always been missing. Andreas had had companions over the years, but no one to whom he felt akin. Being with Clara reminded him of how much a person needs that kind of partnership. Simply being in her presence created a peace within him that justified all the other aspects of his life. He needed that. He needed her. The difficult part would be convincing her that she needed him.

"I don't remember the book's title, but the message is in here." She tapped on her skull three times with a broad smile.

"We men have been trying to get in touch with our emotional side for years...just for this kind of moment." He dipped his head to the side to see if he had gone too far. After all, he had only just met her.

Clara didn't seem rattled, but simply integrated his comment in the same way she processed all new information.

"Is that okay?" he asked.

"Yes, I think it might be."

CHAPTER TWENTY-FOUR

"Mom, did you read this article?" Adira held her phone up, displaying the writing to her mother.

"That's not an article; it's trash." Their difference in accents had always been a point of humor for them. "Who's this G-A-D fellow you keep talking about?" her mother would ask and Adira would playfully reply, "Oh my *GOWD*, Mom!" They would laugh together.

"I know, but it keeps my mind off reality, and sometimes that's all I want." Adira began reading aloud:

Rattling the Cage of Faith

Three days ago, we all felt the reverberations of the tragic shooting on the soil of an American military base. The nature of tragedy isn't debatable. Not when the death toll hit thirteen and thirty-two others were injured. However, our sources have found that there is more to this story.

Late Tuesday afternoon, the shooter was taken down by two unidentified individuals. In fact, reports say that the two non-military men must have each taken a single shot simultaneously since two distinct shells were found lodged in the shooter's spine. Although he survived the onslaught, the victim will be paralyzed from the waist down. In turn, he is awaiting his trial.

Even though the guards on base were sure that the non-military "saviors" checked in at the station, no record of their existence remains. They showed identification, which all guards at their posts conveniently forgot in the chaos of the moment, and no record of their entrance remains.

Witnesses say they saw a civilian woman leave the compound with the two men before police were able to detain them for questioning. Some believe they saw blood trailing behind one of the men. This begins the strand of endless questions. Who was this woman? She did not check in at the post with any guards. Why did they leave before the police were able to take a statement? This doesn't seem to follow any pattern of heroic behavior. How did these men bring weapons onto a military base with strict security designed for such things not to happen? Were they in league with the shooter and is it possible that they left him for dead when they decided he was expendable? Maybe he is the innocent one after all, taking the fall for those who have fallen from grace. Lastly, how is it possible that if one of these men had been shot, he was not, in turn, treated at a nearby hospital? No record of gunshot wound victims matching their descriptions was located that day or those that followed.

Maybe, just maybe, these so-called heroes, painted as such by other media sources, aren't heroes at all. Too many questions have gone unanswered. This writer pleads that these three unknown individuals come forward to answer them.

"I am so tired of biased media. Whatever happened to news? What happened to journalistic integrity? I mean, who cares who these guys are? They came in and took down the assailant before he could kill others. They say these guys may have saved upwards of fifty lives. They say this shooter had that much ammo in his bag. And now, they are being crucified because they are media sell-outs? Give me a break." Adira slammed the phone down in disgust.

"I told you not to read it. It's trash."

"I know that it is trash, but it's like a car wreck; you can't help but look at it."

"Oh, I can help it all right."

Adira couldn't help but love her mother's thick New York accent. She hadn't lived in Long Island for forty years now, but that accent never faded. Their relationship had, though. Because of Adrian.

Adira's mom had known that Adrian was dark from the beginning.

Adira had brought him home not long after meeting him. She was seventeen; Adrian twenty. That age difference was a problem from the start. It was stereotypical: she was enamored by his college stories and apathetic nature. He'd been arrested more than once, but Adira desperately believed in him and defended him when he said he was simply in the wrong place at the wrong time. Thinking back on it now, it was hard not to chastise herself for her own stupidity. He had gotten off easily since he was a minor and had no priors, but just because it was his first, it didn't mean it would be his last. Or just because he had been caught didn't mean that it really was his first. Regardless of the knowledge she had gained as the years passed, Adira had thought he was the most charismatic man she'd ever met. But all the fighting with her mom after her dad had been killed had finally pushed her out the door.

On this day, however, she looked at her mother and thought about how she couldn't imagine a life without her. She had been a rock when Tommy had been diagnosed and hadn't stopped that support even after his death.

But back then, she and her mother couldn't have been any more different. Where Adira faded, her mother sparkled. Adira's priorities were so very different from her mother's that it made for a fight over every topic. This wasn't just negotiating, which Adira later learned was a part of parenting; this was an all-out fight every time. And each time they fought, Adira pulled a little farther away.

And Adrian was waiting right there for her.

Looking back on it now, Adira still clung to the hope that she hadn't been so wrong about it. She still believed there had been love there. She had to believe, for Tommy's sake, that love had brought him into her life. But where once there may have been love, it had slowly been replaced by something vastly different.

People tend to argue over the definition of the true opposite of love. Whether it is hate or apathy, Adira hadn't entirely determined. But she knew quite desperately that both of those emotions had scuttled into her heart when thinking about the father of her child. She hadn't known how or when the darkness had swept in—maybe it had always been there—but it emerged quite suddenly and with a closed-fisted certainty.

Years later, after having left the only house that she'd known, married a mystery man in Las Vegas, birthed her beautiful baby boy, and been beaten to the edge of life to protect that boy, she finally spoke to her mother.

"People are born with both a dark and a light side," her mother had said. "Everyone has the capability of throwing over that balance. Adrian always had that dark side. You just made the choice not to see it. Love blinds a person." She had tried to comfort Adira. She wasn't trying to tell her that she knew all along; she simply wanted to make it clear that she understood. And how desperately Adira had needed to hear that!

Those words, however, haunted Adira on this day. Did she have a dark side? Because the moment she had seen the bruises on Tommy, she had known it was Adrian. And when she had seen them, she had wanted to kill the man she had once loved. Was that the darkness her mother had spoken about? When Adrian had come after them with fury in his eyes because they'd left him, she would have done anything to protect her child. Was that darkness? Was the fear she felt when they hid in motel after motel part of that darkness? How about when she wanted to deck the doctor after he had diagnosed Tommy with cancer? Was that it? Or the rage she felt when she knew it was the end and there wasn't a goddamn thing she could do about it? Or what did it say about her that she had felt relieved that moment she realized that Tommy had taken his last breath? What kind of mother thinks that?

She was beginning to think that her mother was right. Maybe there was something about that darkness that was seducing her.

Adira wasn't sure if she was strong enough to stop it without Tommy.

CHAPTER TWENTY-FIVE

"*W*hat are you doing?" Andreas slid with ease into the chair beside Clara. The desk at which she sat was cluttered with screens, papers, and books concerning technology and research spanning centuries.

"A little light reading..." She held up a dusty volume covered with yellowed-brown leather.

"What is that?" Andreas asked as he ran his fingers over the leather cover. He delicately turned the first few pages. Raising his head, he caught Clara's chin. He needed no excuse to touch her. "Can you read this?"

"It's the Rigveda. And yes, I taught myself the written language this morning."

"What language is this?"

"Vedic Sanscrit."

Andreas could not help but be amazed by this woman. His emotions clashed between a need to protect her and a feeling of reverence toward her.

Clara retrieved the text from him in a huff of intolerance. "It just so happens that this is one of the oldest sacred texts still circulating the globe. It's based in Hinduism. I was thinking this morning that the best place to start is to look at the existing human religions. If you look at the most consistent reason that humanity has divided itself over the years, it is due to religion. The Poneros have been corrupting those belief systems since the beginning of time. Most conflicts are rooted in the justification of some religious sect claiming a higher morality. How can I understand where the problems are and anticipate more of these conflicts without better understanding other religions? Hinduism is considered the oldest living one, so I thought I would start there."

Andreas picked up a tablet and scrolled through the information, enjoying the furrow in Clara's brows as she worked. "With one billion followers, most live in India; it's the third largest religion next to Islam and Christianity."

"Yep..." Clara had moved on while not listening to the man beside her. He tried not to take insult.

"And it says here that followers worship at the altar of Clara because her beauty is unparalleled..." He actually put his finger on the paper, pretending to read.

Without looking up, Clara commented, "Really? Does that work on the other women here?"

"I wouldn't know. I've never tried it on anyone else. It felt a little cheesy coming out though. How did it sit with you?" She laughed, and that was all he had striven for. He worried about her after they'd left each other last night. He'd settled her into her new apartment, stark of anything but research, and as he'd walked to his own dwelling, he was unsettled by the feeling that all of this might be too much for her.

Clara couldn't help laughing at his flirtations. She was adjusting to this new life, this new purpose, probably this new body (she had no idea), but she didn't want to add a romantic layer to whatever all of this was. She enjoyed his company, there was no doubt. She liked the innocent flirtations. They were a reprieve from the constant pressure to find answers, but anything more might make for more questions, and that was a risk she just couldn't take now.

As if feeling her hesitation, he returned his gaze to the screens in front of him. The one at which she was looking showed excerpts from the Rigveda. "You have some highlighted," he noted. "'Ego is the biggest enemy of humans. When there is harmony between the mind, heart and resolution then nothing is impossible.' Why these? Are you trying to tell me something? I think I've kept my ego in check pretty well so far..."

She ignored his light tone with a wispy smile and asked, "What do you think?" She turned it on him. Cowardly, she thought, of herself, but she was cognizant of being too flustered to respond just yet. And, honestly, she valued his opinion. Having spent little more than a day with him, she felt connected to him in a way she couldn't quite understand.

"Well, from what I know of Hinduism...which I learned in the last ten minutes...it is a belief system that has been evolving for the better part of the last ten thousand years or so. They are the initiators of karma and all that." It was the first time since Andreas's transformation that he'd felt inadequate. Sure, he had failed at many missions, and succeeded in just as many, but he had never wanted something as much as he wanted Clara's approval. He needed it, in some juvenile way, and each moment with her, although comfortable, still felt like a kind of test. He needed to prove himself.

"Yes. Although, that was much later, karma, reincarnation and personal enlightenment and transformation are at the heart of what modern Hindus believe." She continued, rattling off all she'd learned. It felt good to expel information. It was almost as if it was necessary to let out as much as she was taking in. "Between the fifth and ninth centuries of the Common Era, Buddhists and Hindus flourished together. Then, something pulled Hindus away from Buddha; Buddhists declined as Islamic rule forced most to convert. Really, through all that turmoil, it's amazing that either survived."

Clara stopped for a moment to catch her breath. She'd felt sometimes during the last forty-eight hours that her mind often moved too quickly for her mouth to keep up. It was equally annoying and exhausting. Her mind could now access information through a series of visual signs. When a question was posed, her mind accessed the information like a computer code which she tracked visually. The answer presented itself through the translation of that code. "It wasn't until much later that Hindus developed these concepts, but they have always maintained the view of including all. There's beauty in that belief that most people don't recognize, don't you think? The concept of having a strong belief system and yet not excluding others."

Nodding, while reading off of another screen, Andreas found, "'Indian philosophers came to regard the human as an immortal soul encased in a perishable body and bound by action, or karma, to a cycle of endless existences.' Hmm...that sounds familiar. I have never asked Elpis if I am stuck in a cycle that is bound to continue recycling."

Her lips drew in to pause and then she spoke nonchalantly, "Is there a reason you haven't asked? What do you believe?" Her entire focus was on him now, which wasn't her usual way. Often she could accomplish many tasks at once, and he occasionally felt like a small boy vying for his mother's attention, but not now.

"It isn't so much that I haven't asked, but more that I trust in what I cannot understand. That is blind faith, I know." It was the first time Andreas had put words to many of the thoughts he'd had over the years. Although he and Elpis had spoken endlessly about the complexities of their existence, he had found that not all the answers lay before them. There were many times when he felt that Elpis was holding something back.

They had spoken of their pasts, at length. Sometimes Andreas felt he needed to talk about his human days. He wanted to keep the memories fresh, when all that had happened to him here had threatened to replace them with some new mission. Much of who he was here could not have happened without his human memories.

Yet, he often wondered about Elpis. Occasionally, his friend would reference time periods, dates, or events that placed him at the heart of a world history that, to Andreas, had always remained closed within a book. Elpis was the oldest Go'El in existence. Andreas knew that, but he didn't know what had kept him so long. Was he waiting for something?

Having unanswered questions between them had become the norm. For Andreas, it was refreshing to maintain a close relationship with someone on the other end of the journey. Andreas liked being the one to travel it with Clara.

"And you're okay with that? Not having answers?"

"How can I not be? I died. I can recall my life, remember? If that experience doesn't teach you about faith, I don't know what will."

Clara looked at the man before her. In his mid to late thirties, his skin was not mired by age so much as enhanced by it. His black hair was peppered with gray that gave him the distinction of experience. Her eyes traveled down his slightly crooked nose; a fracture, she thought, that had probably healed too quickly. But it lent him a realism that somehow comforted her. He was beautiful in a way only a man can be, but that crooked nose made her feel less self-conscious about her own imperfections. Imperfections she was still only beginning to know. His lips, permanently raised in a slight smile, encouraged Clara toward humor. She often found herself staring at them during their conversations, unwilling to lift her eyes.

Andreas wore his clothes; they did not wear him. Outwardly, he appeared strong, but not in a Leonidas sort of way, even though she had read the reports. She knew that in reality Andreas could reduce the Spartan to dust, yet he wasn't intimidating. Clara had no doubt that he was a good man.

"What happened to you? I mean, I read your files...I hope you don't mind...I know the basics, but, I want to hear your story."

"You read my files? What did they say?" Andreas's eyes widened with concern, not anger. She wondered briefly where the concern was rooted.

"I didn't read deeply; just the cover sheets. It felt intrusive, yet hollow. I only took what I needed in order to move forward in my understanding of the Go'El and your capabilities for a mission."

Andreas hesitated and looked at the woman before him, debating how to answer the question she had laid out.

"What are you afraid to tell me? I know about the cancer...the smoking. Is that it? Are you afraid that I will know you're an idiot? Yes, I think you're an idiot for smoking. Your family must have wanted to kill you."

He couldn't help but laugh...at more than just the directness of her words. His body bounced with the lightness of her tone, yet the insults had pitted him. Mostly, he felt the relief that it was his story to tell, not a report in a file. "Yes, I was an idiot."

Clara returned the smile but waited patiently. There was more; she knew he wanted to say more. "Are you afraid because you think your memories might hurt me more for not having any of my own?"

His eyes closed slightly, as if her words had pained him. "I smoked. I got cancer. I ended up here. What else do you want to know?" He knew that he was stalling...and being a bit of an ass about it. But he simply didn't know where to start, or how.

"I just want to know about you," Clara said quietly, eyes turned down. And for the first time since he'd entered the room, they were not focused on papers or screens, but on her hands. She looked so innocent that he wanted to hold her. His fingers twitched with need, but he held back, too afraid to rush her. "I have no memories of my own. I just want to know yours, and not the things that I can read in a file. It is hard not to focus on the negative when you look at a file. That is human nature, I guess, to see the worst. But then, I'm with you and my shoes are off and I can smell the sunshine and... It's that! *Smelling* the sunshine. That doesn't make logical sense. But it's there, and it makes me realize that there is so much beauty that people don't see. At least, they rarely write about it. So I want to hear about your beautiful memories. I want to know everything."

He thought about what this must be like for her. They'd spoken of blind faith before and here she was with no memory to ground her to a world that seemed to change beneath their feet every day. He needed to anchor her to something, but he just didn't know how. So, he told her his story.

"I grew up in The States, but my parents were from Greece." He waited for a second to see if there would be any reaction, but also to buy him time. Although his mind raced with avenues down which he could take his story, some that bypassed specific memories, he struggled with which one to take. "I had a sister, whom I adored. She was younger and was devastated when I enlisted during the second war. I got in late, saw a little action. I was a navy man. I'd dropped out of school to enlist with the thought of going back after the war. But I met a woman." He traced an outline on his forearm, fingering a tattoo of an anchor that had once adorned his skin. Now, that finger followed an empty path.

"My life started and ended with her.

"I was on leave, about to be honorably discharged. Some buddies of mine were heading to a place to dance and drink. We liked to drink a good amount back then, and for me, it didn't take much. But I hadn't had one on the night I saw her. She had been leaving; I was coming in. It was late, snow had layered the Chicago streets and I know it's contrite to say that she looked like an angel, but that is the perfect comparison. She had a white coat with a fur collar that hugged her shoulders, and as her hair dropped in thick curls around it, she was smiling. She always smiled, except when she was angry at me, but even then I could make her smile with some ridiculous joke or a tickle behind her knee." He was silent for a moment, whether he waited for a reaction from Clara or a need to settle his own emotions which were more intense than he had anticipated, he wasn't sure. But his eyes never left her. They never drifted to the scene he was describing. Instead, they bore into her as if forcing her full attention. Clara seemed consumed by his words as they fell around her like raindrops that she studied closely on the way down.

"Anyway, I grabbed her arm on her way out and she didn't lose her smile; she just turned to me with curiosity. Like I was a new adventure for her and I just didn't know it yet. We danced all night long. I knew she had to be mine.

"She was so afraid of being late that she begged me to let her go. Unlike any girl I'd known, she was going to university. Most women of that generation weren't remotely thinking of doing that. Her parents were divorced and her father lived in Chicago, but her mother was still overseas. She lived with her aunt, with whom she didn't want to get into trouble because she desperately wanted to finish her education." He felt his words flow out of him at lightning speed, but he couldn't help it. Memories like these exhilarated him. It was a reminder of how lucky he had been and what it had taken to get here. Clara was right; memories were magic.

"She had played it cool, trying to leave without my telephone number, or without giving me hers... After I asked numerous times, she finally gave me the address to her dorm at the university. But she told me that if I were to write her, it would have to be under the name of her roommate, for fear of her aunt.

"So I wrote her every day, sometimes more than once a

day. Our souls spilled onto the paper. We found each other and ourselves in those words in a way that I'm not sure people do when they are face to face. Sometimes, it's easier to become vulnerable on paper. I often wonder what happened to those letters.

"I finished my tour. She finished for the year and I took her out the very first night that I could and we stood under the stars looking at the lake with the city backdrop behind us. I told her I loved her. I told her I had spent my life wondering if love like this existed, and now that I knew that it did, I wanted it forever.

"Cliché, I know. But sometimes love does that.

"We were married one month later. We had two beautiful girls. We traveled. We laughed. We cried. We screamed. But, God, we loved each other.

"And then I got sick. And I can't think of what it did to her. But here I am. And I don't...I can't regret any of it."

CHAPTER TWENTY-SIX

"*W*ho's next?"

Twelve hands shot into the air, fingers wiggling for attention as Elaina smiled at the enthusiasm in her classroom. Nothing was more exhilarating for her than when her class not only comprehended a topic quickly, but was eager to discuss it.

"Talk to me, George." She bent her finger, indicating they should switch seats.

"I brought in this article about Thomas Jefferson. He is a great example of how we, as a society, like to make heroes of certain people. I understand that Jefferson was a hero in his own way during a difficult time, but..."

"Slow down, George. Make your claim."

"The 'heroification', as Mr. Loewen terms in his book, *Lies My Teacher Told Me,* of Thomas Jefferson is unsubstantiated." George took a breath and looked at his teacher.

"Clear claim. What's your evidence?" Elaina replied.

"Well, historians believe that he was one of the greatest United States presidents of all time. He was an author of the Constitution, and he opposed slavery for the better part of his adult life. Mrs. T., he has one of the coolest looking monuments in Washington." George was pleading a bit, but she loved it when the kids impressed her with a unique line of thought.

"Okay, you've justified that he has been 'heroified', but now I need you to support your claim. Why shouldn't he be?"

"Well, for one thing, he owned hundreds of slaves. How can you oppose something that you are participating in? I mean, I am not going to say 'smoking is bad, no one should do it' while I have a cigarette hanging out of my mouth."

"No, that would be hypocritical," Elaina agreed, hoping for more.

"But, did you know that not only did Jefferson own slaves, but after his wife died, he supposedly got it on with her half-sister who was the daughter of Jefferson's wife's father...and a slave? Yep, and Jefferson had a kid with her. But they can't refer to Sally Hemings (that was her name) as a common law wife. They never got married, because Martha, Jefferson's wife that died (and Sally's half-sister) asked him not to marry again. So, he didn't. But, after DNA testing in 1998, they found that Sally had had a baby and that the child was most likely Jefferson's. So history remembers her as Jefferson's concubine (since she was a half child of a slave). All of that is pretty messed up, I'd say. So, Jefferson is not a hero!"

"Interesting research... Sounds like a celebrity wives show on TV." Elaina walked back to the front of the room to return to her chair. George stood, took a bow in response to some sparse clapping, and returned to his seat as well.

"What do you think about that story? What did you learn that you didn't know before? What do you think of George's claim?" Elaina looked from eye to eye as she searched for that spark of recognition from someone who might just see what she was seeing. It was so hard not to lecture as a teacher. She desperately wanted to just give the answer, but she knew that they had to see it themselves.

A hand shot up in the back of the room. "Hiba, what are you thinking?"

"Well, I think that we, as people, like to 'heorify' others because we need some level of hope. But there are just as many people who tear down those heroes, and they thrive off that satisfaction, I guess." Hiba looked sorrowful in her statement. This seemed personal. Elaina had found that the best answers so often were.

"That's an interesting observation. What do the rest of you think? Can you think of evidence where that is true?"

To her astonishment, a few hands rose. "Muhammad, what do you think?"

"I agree with Hiba. Look at this year's Wimbledon," he said.

"Now you're speaking my language," Elaina said.

"I thought you'd like that. But seriously, Andy Murray won one of the greatest Grand Slams of all time. He was the first British person to take the title in seventy-seven years. But what article stood alone the following morning? 'Murray Forgets to Thank His Mum'. Really? Give the guy a break. He'd just attained his lifelong goal. Sorry, he needed a minute...and he did thank her. It just took him a minute."

"Great example. Current event. I like it. Tennis oriented...even better. Can anyone think of any figures in ancient history where we've built them up or torn them down, both a little too audaciously?"

"Jesus!" Mikey shouted.

"Thank you for raising your hand, Mikey," Elaina replied with a roll of her eyes. "Go on."

"Jesus was built up and torn down. I mean, regardless of what you believe, he was a man seen as the Messiah. Whether you believe it or not, I don't think he was hurting anyone. He was preaching good lessons. Lessons most other religions were not arguing at the time. But because people felt threatened by the thought that it was possible that their belief system was wrong or that people might think they were wrong, they crucified him." Mikey toyed with the cross on his chest. There were questions behind that comment that Elaina didn't feel comfortable pursuing that day. But the kids were thinking. That was a great thing!

"Interesting justifications; I like the way you are thinking. Anyone else?"

"The Prophet Muhammad was hunted most of his life. Some say he was poisoned. And even after his death at the age of sixty-something, people tried to decimate his grave," one child related.

"Another good example. Tell me more."

The same child continued, "Well, it's like what Mikey said. People are afraid of things that force them to question what they believe. And the Prophet Muhammad even acknowledged the sanctity of Jesus. He didn't claim to be the only one of his kind. They taught similar lessons, carried a similar belief system. But people tried to tear him down anyway."

Another student raised her hand. "What about the Jews?"

"Sarah, what about them?" Elaina responded.

"Well, we've been persecuted for our beliefs for as long as history has been recorded. I mean...talk about slaves. Who do you think built the pyramids? The Coliseum? The Jews were enslaved because of their beliefs."

"All good points, and I like the connection to slavery, but we are getting away from our heroes. Who are they? Why do we create them and tear them down?" Elaina caught the hands of the clock out of the corner of her eye, satisfied with the progression of the conversation.

"I think that people will inevitably remember heroes after they've died, probably sacrificing themselves for the greater good. But, before that... Well, change is scary. And any time someone emerges and makes us question ourselves, well, I just don't think humans are evolved enough to handle it. Fear drives us." The bell rattled all the teenagers to their feet in a hustle of books and chatter.

"We will talk more tomorrow," said Elaina, dismissing them as they filed out. She was left with the echo of those last words. *Fear drives us.* The scariest part about that sixteen-year-old's words was that they were true. And that's what worried Elaina.

CHAPTER TWENTY-SEVEN

Tom awoke the following day with no bumps or bruises, no sore muscles or strained ligaments. The training he had had the day before, however, had been his most grueling. The simulator had erased from his mind his most sacred possession—memories of his mother.

The hologram had looked so real. It had all felt so real. Even though every part of his being fought the concept that it was her who needed saving, he couldn't help but react.

Tommy, I need you. He found us.

He felt the sweat surface on his upper lip and a tremor anchored in anger, not fear, ran through his body. He could process with certainty that this was just another test. He had passed the rest with flying colors. He had taken down the target in his first real head to head with the Poneros.

But he couldn't detach from this event the way he had the others.

I tried to hide you. I tried not to leave a trail. I don't know how he found us. He left this note: "You're my family. Whatever I have done is in the past. You owe me another try. He's my son."

Mom, I'm stronger now. We can face him together. He can't hurt us anymore.

Tom struggled with the words he knew weren't accurate. He was stronger, yes, but not invincible. He could face him, but only with his mother.

As part of being initiated into the Go'El, Tom knew the rules. Through their reincarnation, they were not allowed to interact with any aspect of their old lives, at least not deliberately. If, through a mission, an interaction were to occur, protocols were in place that would minimize the emotional disruption it might cause.

People are not ready to understand the truth, Tom thought to himself.

When the war began, rules were determined for reincarnates. The original Go'El were victims of cancer, and the initiation into the world of the Go'El changed their physical appearance to such an extent that families would have little chance of recognizing them.

Tom knew this when he saw his mother. He knew that he looked nothing like the eight-year-old boy that Adira had buried. And still the reunification intrigued him. He wanted it to be real.

Tommy's father emerged from the shadows. Tom stiffened at his father's appearance. A response he'd learned during childhood, his first inclination was to hide. Even now, in this place and in this body, knowing on some level that this wasn't real, he still could not stop the feeling.

He looked the same. Tom's memory of him was no longer a child's memory; it had sharpened. With deepening facial lines, he had aged more than his forty-two years. His blonde hair was dark now, no whisper of the sun-kissed surfer that had attracted Adira. He had angry streaks of gray, like lightning bolts, that reminded Tom of the suddenness of his fury.

"Adrian, always a pleasure to see you..." Adira stood, pushing her shoulders back in defiance.

"Adira, you never wore sarcasm well."

Tom took a step in front of Adira; no longer would he cower in fear behind her. "Mom, this is my fight now."

"I'm not leaving. I left you alone with him too many times."

What kind of a man could hate his own child?

The Poneros.

And then it clicked. This man, his father, was a member of the Poneros. But was this just an untidy circumstance made real through the simulation? Or had Tom's father always been part of the evil that he was now fighting against?

He took a step backward, widening his stance, waiting for the coming onslaught. He always liked to let the first hit come. As Andreas had taught him, it was like watching the first strike. That one concession taught one so much about his opponent. Was he fighting from rage or fear? Was he clear-headed or confused? The crack of his lip didn't faze him at all as he took in the needed information. But as he faced his opponent, he heard the sounds behind him that instantly chilled his blood.

He turned to Adira, knowing immediately that he had let down his guard like the rookie he was trying so desperately not to be. The blow bit into his eye, like the crack of a whip, and he struggled to find his balance and clear his vision.

Adira's hands shook as she attempted to unhook the device that was counting down on her chest. She clawed at her back trying to get away from the danger.

"Mom, stop!" Blood splattered from Tom's split lip as he yelled. "There's a fail-safe on the buckle on your back. If you unhook it, the bomb will explode." His calm tone belied his volcanic nerves.

Silence fell over them

2:57...2:56...2:55

"*Disengage it—now!*" Tom turned to his father as he spoke, trying to gain composure and ignore the need to tear the man limb from limb.

It occurred to him as he stood and squared his shoulders to recover from the sucker punch that he looked just like his father. They were standing eye to eye in a standoff that reverberated years of panic and abuse. Adrian's eyes glittered with the high he always generated from gaining the upper hand. His sadist whisperings surrounded him with every word and every action. Still, his features were the same as the man Tom had so recently grown accustomed to seeing in the mirror each day. Not an exact replica, but close. Adrian didn't realize it, or at least he hadn't acknowledged it, so focused he'd been on destruction.

Take the right road, not the simple one.

Looking into those shark's eyes, Tom wanted to tear the arms that had beaten his mother from the man's body. "Disengage it, now!" he commanded again.

"Even if I could, which I can't, what would be the point? You can't win. You never could. You have always been helpless; with me, with your mother, even fighting cancer. Just give in to it. You're on the wrong side."

Leaning forward only slightly, Tom discerned how muddled his mind had become. Whether from the sharp blow or the simulation, he was not manipulating information the way he normally did. This isn't real, he thought to himself. It is only a simulation. Focus. Stay focused. Disengage weapon, eradicate target, ameliorate the victim.

Tom contemplated the order in which he would proceed. First, he determined that his father had no weapons or triggers on his person. He couldn't allow him to be a distraction to himself or his mother.

And he'd been waiting years to do this.

Moving more quickly than Adrian's vision could assimilate, Tom swept his left leg cleanly beneath his father's limbs, knocking him to the floor. With the heel of his right hand, Tom popped the pressure point on his father's temple. It wasn't a particularly hard hit, but it was clean, and his father fell limply to the floor. There, he would remain unconscious for long enough to deal with the bomb.

"Is he dead?" she asked.

"No, he'll come around. Let's take care of this before he does." Tom swept his hands over the weapon, familiarizing himself with the model.

He had seen it before in training.

No one had ever successfully disarmed this type of weapon.

His thoughts returned to his training. As if flipping through the pages of a book, his mind raced to find an alternative to ensure their survival.

1:03...1:02...1:01

Adira pointed to the slumped figure on the tile floor.

"There are too many people in this building. I have to get out of here and find somewhere to minimize the damage." Mind galloping, Tom remembered his training: *Minimize casualties. If there is no option for saving all lives, find a way to minimize casualties.*

The concept of sacrifice has been intertwined with religion since the first pictures of organized religion emerged on Egyptian walls. And to this day, the concept has stayed firmly rooted in most belief systems.

The notion of heroism is deeply valued across all cultures. However, within its truest definition, there is symmetry. It must be voluntary, but if it is taught and valued, is that voluntary? It must be done in the service of people in need, but who determines whose needs are most important? It involves a level of risk, whether it be physical or social or in terms of affecting one's quality of life. Still, who determines what the level of risk should be?

Herein lies the question for a Go'El. Is sacrifice the ultimate meaning behind existence? If sacrificing pieces of oneself or oneself in entirety is done so that others may live a more prosperous life, how can it be done selflessly?

Wouldn't any good person gain some peace from knowing that he is sacrificing so that others may flourish? But if he has lived a life worth living, wouldn't he fight to maintain it rather than destroy?

Jesus's sacrifice was considered ultimate. Holiness in Christianity is so often intertwined with self-sacrifice and following the path that Jesus took. Sacrifice is also at the very heart of the Islamic faith. The Qur'an says, "Verily my worship, my sacrifices, and my life and death are wholly dedicated to Allah, Lord of the Worlds." Equally important, the Torah follows a similar line of thought. In fact, the Hebrew word for sacrifice is *korban* which comes from the same verb as *karev* meaning "to come close". This is interpreted that the only way to "become close" to our Creator is to channel our energies into more Godly pursuits; and sacrificing is one of those.

But one did not have to look far to see that these interpretations of self-sacrifice had been manipulated by the Poneros over time; there has been all manner of destruction in the name of a higher power. When is sacrifice simply insanity? Tom thought about the lessons that he had been taught throughout his training; the hours that he and Banko had poured over their tablets looking for patterns in Poneros behavior.

There were no patterns, only chaos. And chaos is unpredictable.

Banko had been particularly disturbed by the more than one hundred Tibetan Buddhists who had set themselves ablaze in order to protest Chinese policies. Tom was struck at how the term 'suicide bomber' has become a staple in any evening news report. It is a term that is as common as 'working class' these days. But even in protests against the Catholic Church, the Northern Irish continued their hunger strike, even after people died from self-starvation. Where was the Poneros in that? Who was sacrificing whom, and for what?

Knowing that he was being tested in the simulation

with his mother, Tom struggled to remove the emotion from his decision making. The problem with such scenarios was that there weren't clear winners and losers. There simply was no right or wrong. This was guerrilla warfare, and the Poneros were just better at fighting dirty.

If Tom left his mother to run from the building to find an empty field and sacrifice herself, then she would save others, but lose her life...alone. Tom wasn't sure he could live with himself after that, even during a simulation. He knew he would never let that happen in reality and needed to stay true to that. If he let her go, the probability that she would save members of the population was very low. Regardless, he knew what he needed to do. But could he really bring his own mother to her death? Bending the iron from a chair back, like an overstretched balloon, he folded the black rod and wrapped it around his father's hands and ankles, properly immobilizing him. The sinister thought of dropping his elbow one more time to snap the cartilage in Adrian's nose passed quietly through his mind. He shook his head slightly, convincing himself of the need to remain focused.

He gathered his mother into his arms and darted quickly down the two flights of stairs, skipping four at a time. The counter clicked away each second, but with his speed and strength he already knew he would have no problem clearing the population. As he tracked through the nearby trees, he followed the trail to a clearing that would position his mother one mile from onlookers. They might feel the heat of the blast, if the trees didn't completely contain it, but it wouldn't do much more than knock them a foot or two backward.

He looked down at the brave woman in his arms and knew that there was no other place that he would rather be. But that didn't make watching this any easier.

"I love you. And I am so proud of what you have become. I wish that we could have been able to share it together."

"We are sharing in it. This is where we were meant to be."

CHAPTER TWENTY-EIGHT

"*W*e made a call."

"It was the wrong call."

"Okay, so how do we move forward?" Clara looked to her mentor, feeling the bitter reflection of disappointment radiating from him. His emotion was what she feared most. There was a point, she knew, where failing would eat away at her, too. She wasn't sure how long she could take the pressure. Elpis's disappointment tended to unhinge her, although he was never overtly overwrought. His practiced composure had settled her during the last missions so this reaction burdened her already strained mind.

"Elpis, you encouraged the government to focus solely on the passengers. They intensified their screening process. It helped."

"I know, Clara, I know. But we have to pick and choose our battles. People were lashing out because they worried we'd see their underwear through the scanners. Can you imagine that? Yes, undergarments could be seen, and that was a privacy concern, but wouldn't you want the peace of mind that comes with finding the C4 strapped to their..." Elpis stopped and closed his eyes at the intensity of his resentment. He lifted his chin to the ceiling, stretching his neck from side to side.

With a clearing of her throat, she refocused. "Well, here's what we have now," she said as she guided them both back to business. "I think it's in the printer cartridges. They are going to be sent from multiple locations in Yemen to Chicago today. I intercepted some chatter between Saudi Arabian and American intelligence. Send me in."

"I'm not sending you in alone. Who do you want?"

"Andreas." She tried to respond casually but knew she should have at least pretended to contemplate her decision. He was the best; there were no doubt of that. Although, Tom ranked amongst the best in his class in training. And Banko had an intuitive response to all missions that intrigued Clara. But it wasn't with Tom or Banko that she wanted to spend time. Even in that moment, however, she refused to allow herself to admit her reasoning. Andreas really was the most logical choice.

"What was that about you wanting me?" Andreas smiled widely as he walked into the room with his confident stride. Feeling her heart stutter several times, Clara made the decision not to answer. Instead of subduing the attraction, she stared at this man toward whom her feelings had grown far too powerful.

Elpis looked from Clara to Andreas; feeling like he was interrupting a private moment but comprehending too well that time was of the essence. He had to trust that the two would not allow their emotions to get in the way of the mission. "There are two packages. One was dropped off by a twenty-two-year-old engineering student, whom we can only assume is Poneros, at a post office in a large city in Yemen. Another was dropped off a few blocks from the original location by a different Poneros on the same day. Both packages have a final destination of Chicago. However, they have already made multiple stops in different cities. The only place where they will find common ground will be their final destination. We don't believe they will detonate until that point. We have to intervene before they arrive in Chicago."

"According to the information I have intercepted," Clara continued, finally composed, "it sounds like they are homemade bombs packaged as printer cartridges. From what I am seeing, I think they may explode mid-air above Chicago. Right now, I'm not sure of the motive, other than iterating a symbol of power and fear by the Poneros."

"There aren't many passengers on Cargo flights, right?" Andreas questioned, turning his full attention to the tablet at his disposal.

"No, that's what worries me. What are we missing? I mean, any human life should be saved, but it seems out of character for the Poneros to be taking aim at a mid-flight cargo plane. Do you think they could get close enough to Willis Tower or Trump?"

"Sears Tower, not Willis...it will always be the Sears Tower." Andreas retorted without looking up.

"What's their no-fly zone policy?" Elpis asked as he looked up the answers himself.

Clara responded with amazing precision. "After September 11th, there was a no fly policy in the downtown to protect the buildings that were known targets, but they only enforce that stringent policy during high profile events like the NATO summit. They have the Air and Water Show, which would increase radar use, but we aren't anywhere near that time of year. It's possible, but still unlikely." Clara shook her crossed ankle repetitively as she leafed through pages on her tablet. Andreas couldn't help but smile at her idiosyncrasies.

"We need to intercept them. Let's stop trying to respond to the event as it is already in progress and stop them from happening altogether. That's why Clara is here. Once this becomes public, there is going to be a level of panic again, akin to the aftermath of September 11th."

Andreas opened the drawer in the desk. He produced several IDs and handed one to Clara. She watched him patch his weapon to the holster hidden underneath his vest, and a knife slid inside his right boot.

Her hands paused with the reality of what was coming. She'd had little to no physical training and was being thrown into a potentially catastrophic mission.

"Do we at least have a destination?" asked Andreas.

"We have two," Clara responded. She was aware that any wrong decision on her part meant the possible loss of a human life, and possibly that of a particular Go'El that she was not ready to sacrifice. Breathing deeply, she responded. "London and Dubai."

"Where to first, doll?" Andreas picked up Clara's coat from the back of her chair and slid it over her arms, letting his hands linger on her shoulders while he waited for the answer. His nonchalance over the pending mission was comforting to her, even though she was fully aware that Andreas was putting on a façade for her benefit. She knew it the minute his fingers touched her. It was a small gesture, but she understood it to be one of encouragement. This unspoken language they had so quickly created with one another was both frightening and exhilarating. She couldn't imagine going on the mission with anyone else.

"We have to go to Britain. I think the United States officials in Dubai are at the airport now, and they should have no problem locating the packages. Only one flight bound for Chicago is scheduled at this time of day. But the UK is already blushing at the fact that it is taking so long to locate the package." Clara opened her ID, noticing it was different than the one she had taken with her to the military installation.

No one can track me because I don't exist, she thought to herself as she tucked it into her small bag that she kept hidden beneath her coat. "I'm not trained for this." It was more an observation than a fearful response, even though she was feeling both.

"I know; we haven't had time, and honestly, we are all new to this. I wasn't even sure if you should be trained, being that you don't have the same...attributes as the Go'El. But..." Elpis drifted off, feeling uncomfortable that he was sending Clara into a hot zone without any more protection than Andreas.

"I won't let anything happen to her. But I need her to locate the package as quickly as possible. I'm fast," Andreas tapped his temple, and then pointed to Clara, "but not that fast." He smiled reassuringly and took her hand. Her finger slipped higher to his wrist and she could feel his heartbeat conflicting with his calm façade. She looked at him a little wide-eyed but did not betray him by speaking. She wasn't sure if the speed by which his heart was beating was due to the mission or to his proximity to her. He, on the other hand, undoubtedly had that effect on Clara.

"We have to move," she said shaking her hand free and marching through the door while trying to detach herself from the abyss of emotion in which she was beginning to drown. Emotion has no place on a mission, she reminded herself.

Andreas hesitated before following her. Before closing the door, he turned back to Elpis. "You know I will protect her. Don't worry so much." He turned away, and then turned back. "And I remember the rules."

The door clicked quietly before the echo of his words faded.

"I know you will," Elpis affirmed. "I know."

CHAPTER TWENTY-NINE

A tear escaped Tom's eye before he could conceal it. He angrily swept it from his cheek and ripped the electrodes from his temples. Slamming his fist on the black button toward the bottom of the screen, he rose abruptly. He knew his reaction was being recorded, and the intimacy of this experience had pushed him over an edge.

Pinching the contacts from his eyes that allowed him to immerse himself visually into a simulation, he placed them into the receptacle. Tom sat back on the chair from which he had jumped when the images of the explosion had shattered him, both physically and emotionally.

The hormones that disperse within a Go'El body while using the special contact lenses allow a subject to receive both visual input through the eyes and emotions transmitted directly to the brainstem via the electrodes. In short, it completely consumes a trainee in a situation, so that logic and strength no longer rule. Without the element of emotion, a Go'El can never truly train for coming deployments.

Today had been the most challenging day of situation training, and Tom was disappointed with his performance.

He had entered the simulation knowing that his training needed to intensify since he had been almost fatally injured on his first mission. He couldn't let that happen again. He wanted desperately to validate the suffering that predicated this existence. Not for personal glory, but to rationalize in some way all the turmoil that he and his mother had endured.

He now acknowledged that all that pain was not without purpose. Indeed, he had saved lives the other day. He had stopped the Poneros from tipping the balance. But it had never occurred to him that because of his position in *this* world, his mother's life might be sacrificed.

"Hey, are you okay?" Banko put her small hand on Tom's back and craned her neck to look into his eyes. Tom had found that whenever he admitted some sort of personal weakness, she would never simply accept his assessment. She saw herself as the mirror which kept him honest with himself.

"No, I'm feeling confused," he admitted.

"Are you coming from the simulator?" She pulled him to the closest bench in the park near their apartments. Prismatic reflections of the springs that surrounded them exuded patterns of color and heat. Their sulfuric aroma danced within his olfactory senses, a comfort in contrast to the nightmare from which he'd emerged. No matter how many days he had spent here, wandering around the national park that he and his mother had sworn to one day visit, he didn't take it for granted. Resting in the most peaceful of places in the world, he now called this place home. Tom and his mother had spent time during his convalescence reading brochures online about all of the national parks they wanted to visit when he finished his treatment.

He remembered how his mom had commented once on it. "Isn't it amazing that the animals in national parks aren't afraid of humans? There are entire generations of species that have never known what it meant to live in fear. That is so awesome!" They had shared that dream. And now he was here, without her.

Shaking his head as the marmots played in the field before him, he finally answered Banko's question. "Yes, I was in the simulator."

Her lips spread wide in waiting.

"My mother," he said.

Banko recoiled. "Was she Poneros?"

"No...no," Tom quickly responded not having considered that that might be how Banko would interpret his reaction.

"Oh, good," she exhaled with relief. He adored her ability to empathize with others. She hadn't known Tom's mother, of course. She hardly knew Tom. But she looked disheartened by Tom's visceral reaction to the simulator. She nudged him with her right shoulder.

Tom had rarely seen Banko sit still. She seemed to be continually pondering the world and the players within it. "No, it's fine. It's just...well, it was the first time I'd seen my mom since..."

"And you've been thinking a lot about her, so that couldn't have been easy."

"Yeah, plus my dad was there."

"Your dad, too? What was that like?" Banko's eyes widened, taking in his every reaction. Then she looked past him for a moment, focused more on her own thoughts than his. "They were testing your ability to handle emotional stress, hence your mom. And they threw your dad in there for a catechism of trials. He tests your ability to remain calm. He invites you to give into your anger and tip your personal balance. He claims your capacity to focus. No wonder you looked disoriented when you came out."

"All of that. But it was worse. In the simulation, he was Poneros, and now that I know what I know, I'm beginning to wonder if the man I remember hadn't been consumed, in reality. In the end, I had to sacrifice my mother...and myself. Honestly, I don't even know if they are going to let me run missions anymore. I can't imagine how my analysis will read."

"You sacrificed your mother and you didn't stop the simulation. That was your final training. Most Go'El take twenty, sometimes thirty training sessions to pass that test. Once we do, we aren't allowed to tell anyone what they entail, but all must pass it. It always involves something personal, and the solution is never simple. They intensify the hormone induction through the contacts so that you are unable to differentiate between the reality of the simulation and the apparent conflict. You passed, Tom! You passed with flying colors!" Banko squeezed his hands, forcing him to mirror her contagious smile.

"Why?" was all Tom could ask.

Banko thought back to her own final simulation. Afterward, she had spoken with Elpis about it and asked the very same question: Why must we sacrifice?

Elpis had calmed her after the emotional upheaval experienced as a result of her trial in the simulator. In hindsight, she wasn't quite sure how or what it was that he had said to push her toward balance, but she wanted to do the same for Tom.

"It's faith, Tom. If you don't have faith, then all of this is for nothing."

CHAPTER THIRTY

"I still haven't quite figured out this whole traveling thing." Clara braced her hands at her sides as they arrived outside London Heathrow Airport. She spoke as she took in the explosion of curves, angles and glass welcoming her to one of the busiest airports in the world. Despite the mission at hand, she was yet again struck by the human experience of simply existing in the moment. She had committed hours of research to memory, most of which revolved around the comings and goings at this airport. Yet no writing can prepare you for what you feel when you see incredible architecture for the first time. The power of an aircraft as it consumes your senses before landing. And the advancing technology that evolves most distinctly in airports from the planes to the advertisements illuminated against endless glass. It was awe-inspiring.

"What do you mean?" Andreas asked as he pulled out his tablet to calculate the best entrance. They had a Go'El stationed as a worker in security. She was going to aid them in their entrance in order to expedite the process.

"I've been curious how we move from place to place. Occasionally we take public transit, but when it is a time sensitive mission, we have the capability to transport from one place to another almost instantly." Rubbing her hands over her eyes, she split her mind to continue the discussion with Andreas while maintaining her commitment to the current mission. "I know about the portals. I was given the Ankh before my first mission to get onto the base, and we are using it again now, but..." Her left hand unconsciously caressed the Egyptian cross and loop artifact in her pocket.

"I've never actually considered the mechanics of the procedure." Andreas stopped her as he knew she would continue postulating. "I just appreciate its flawless functionality. Now, can we get moving? We are on the clock. Jahida is working security. She will get us in quickly. She left this." He picked up a flat piece of what looked like fossilized sand. Andreas handed it to Clara and she ran her fingers over the print that he had so cavalierly handed to her.

Her lashes snapped up immediately in recognition and shock. "This is one of the footprints of the Prophet Muhammad." She gazed down at the artifact in her hand. A left foot, its imprint was definitive but benign. The power behind it was unpronounced. "There are a few of these, but they are in museums. The Muslims believe that the Prophet Muhammad made a lasting impression in and around religious sites in the Middle East. These prints were found years later and preserved."

"And now we use that one as a portal. The Ankh that we have was a particularly compelling artifact, one of the few originals of its time at their inception in Egypt. The cross base with the loop around the top has become a definable characteristic of that lost civilization; it represents birth and rebirth, through the male and female junctures on its symbol. Those artifacts that represent strong ties with God can be used by us as portals to one another. They are rare and we avoid using them because randomly appearing in public areas is frowned upon. Athoos tend to notice when entire humans appear at random. So we used our Ankh to reach Jahida's print. And here we are." Andreas drew her hand in his as he tucked the two artifacts away and moved toward the daunting task ahead.

"Appropriate name," Clara muttered as they quickened their pace through the doors.

"Excuse me?"

"Jahida. Is she Muslim? Her name means 'helps the vulnerable' in Arabic."

Shaking his head at her variability, he continued on his way. "There, she's at the third desk. Stand behind me. Do as I do." Andreas turned abruptly to Clara before entering the line and spoke in a low whisper that blew across her cheek. "Please, stay close. I can't do this if I have to consider for a second that you aren't safe."

The tone of his words sent goose bumps radiating down Clara's arms. Her heart gained wings, while her skin suddenly felt too tight for her body. All she could do was nod.

They approached the desk and Jahida welcomed them both with a masked expression. She gave them quick directions as to where to go next to begin their search. The last thing they wanted to do was to call attention to themselves, especially when Jahida had leaned over and whispered, "Be careful. My radar is definitely going off. The Poneros have clearly infiltrated this system. Someone is working from the inside, and he or she could be here now. Don't trust anyone."

They both dipped their chins in response, eyeing those within earshot. "What do you think? Where is the package?" Andreas pulled Clara closer to him as they worked their way toward one of the many cargo holds.

"Here's the thing: This is the fourth busiest airport in the world. Sixty-six million people come through here every year. At this point, even after the 2007 legislation, only sixty-five percent of the cargo is being x-rayed. And let's be honest, the Poneros have likely found a way to create a bomb that could go through typical scanning processes and sniffing dogs without being detected. In reality, all I can do is track it and hope that you can dismantle it before it is either detonated remotely or you trip some failsafe wire."

"You are so hopeful. I just love that about you," Andreas held his scanner above the boxes being held in cargo.

Inside the holding dock were thousands of identical boxes. Stacked in some cases as high as a story, Clara couldn't conceive of where to begin. She pulled out her tablet and set it to scan.

"We are most likely looking for a printer. I imagine that they wouldn't have simply packed the cartridge. If the explosives were carefully hidden, and the parts of the cartridge were even slightly out of place, a trained scanner would detect that; but if the cartridge was also inside a perfectly intact printer, then it is possible that it made it through the process. Which, clearly it did. This isn't the first stop on the manifesto."

"I love it when you talk manifestos with me," jibed Andreas. Clara was baffled at his ability to remain sharp, but also play a comedic roll. She was beginning to love that about him. Andreas pulled up his scanner and held it above a pile of boxes that appeared to fit the profile size. It was a logical start, but the box was easily one of hundreds.

And they were only examining the first of two loading docks.

"We should split up. There is another room like this, and likely some actual printers being shipped to legitimate destinations. There is no need to scan anything that isn't postmarked for Chicago." Clara moved to the far side of the warehouse.

"Not too far. Stay where I can see you." Andreas continued to filter through the pile in front of him. The boxes weren't grouped together by their final destinations;

they were grouped by their next, which was LaGuardia. This was not going to be easy, and time was ticking away.

Just as they were getting into the groove, one of the large doors opened. "Hey, what are you doing in here?" a baggage handler yelled as Andreas and Clara looked up. She found Andreas's eyes and he could see panic in her expression.

He could be a Poneros at worst. At best, he was taking up too much time by stopping them.

"Hello," Andreas spoke with lightness, quieting his nerves. "It's all right. We've already been through security. We are government officials," he flashed the handler his badge and an easy smile that remained tight with his next words, "and we've been alerted to a suspicious package. We need to take a look around." He was taking a gamble even giving him that much information, but they needed to get back to work and being evasive wasn't going to help. Plus, every hair on his body was leaning toward Clara and the distance that seemed like a chasm. Like magnets, they were each inching closer to one another without even realizing it.

"What kind of package? I'll need to check with my superiors. You'll need to wait." The handler's nervous movements caught Clara's attention. She instantly released her clenched fists, believing him to be an innocent and not a Poneros. When she looked to Andreas, however, it didn't seem that he had let his guard down for a second. She stood still, suggesting to herself that his nerves could simply be an act, or even a response to the assumption that he might possibly be outnumbered. She calculated the space between herself and the potential target as she stood, weaponless, with Andreas separated from her by a sea of boxes and the plausibility of a fight. Her mind instantly catalogued the attendant's body weight and the areas of the body to which she could quickly do the most damage. The eyes, if she could get that close. The neck, if her height estimation was correct. The groin: other soft areas. Smaller combatants, like Clara, needed to optimize her hits.

Andreas's gaze never wavered, but his slight head jerk caught Clara's attention. He was telling her not to relax. They were getting down to minutes, and this might be their only chance.

Andreas had been trained to look for signs that people had been consumed by the Poneros. It had become second nature to him. He examined the stranger from head to toe. He fit the part. Nothing looked out of place. The uniform was pristine. The accent was unfiltered, with a bit of Scottish brogue. All the outward signs suggested he was simply doing the job of a baggage handler.

Clara thought about motives. If he pushes too hard to stall, he could be Poneros. If he offers to help, he could be Poneros. If he turns tuck tail and runs...he's probably Athoos. She waited for his reaction. And she tried to follow Andreas's lead.

She couldn't sit back and wait.

"Sir, I know you are doing your job. But so are we. And one of these packages likely holds an explosive that we have reason to believe will detonate while on board a plane. We need to stop that from happening. We don't have time to talk to you."

Andreas watched him carefully. Looking for the flash that he knew only came before a kill, he readied his hand near his weapon. He was too far from her. How could he protect her without killing the Poneros? He had flashes of a simulation from his past.

Already, he found himself walking toward her. His eyes never left the handler. Andreas abandoned the pile of searchable packages and rerouted his target. He worried the bear was attracted to the alluring scent of food. Andreas was determined to refocus him away from Clara.

He had to get to Clara.

"Tell me what you're looking for and maybe I can help." The handler tucked the rag he'd been wiping his hand with in a back pocket and looked over Clara's shoulder.

He's too close. She's letting her guard down, Andreas realized. Andreas picked up his pace, still aware that he didn't want to alarm a Poneros and force him into action.

Clara took a step toward Andreas, away from the stranger. *Good girl*, he thought. She's smart. She's just as wary.

"I think we are okay right now; we just need to get back to work. If you could head to security and talk to Jahida and inform her of our status, that would be extremely helpful." Clara narrowed her eyes, waiting for the man's response.

They didn't have time for this. But they couldn't take any chances. Andreas and Clara needed to know if he was Poneros. If he didn't attack them now, he could alert others. Time was clicking away.

"Jahida, you say? I think I know who she is. I will need to talk to my superior, too. Cover my arse, ya know? Protocols and all. Do your thing. I won't slow you down." He quickly headed out the door by which he'd arrived, and both Clara and Andreas exhaled a breath they hadn't realized they had been holding.

"That was unnerving," Andreas smiled to calm her.

"Understatement..." Clara blew out another deep breath and pulled her tablet over a pile of Chicago-bound boxes.

"That was smart, what you did. I thought you would ask him to help us. I would have." Andreas quickly resumed the search on the other end, conversing loudly over his shoulder.

"I know." Andreas smiled at her confidence. "I could have done either. Both would have been a decent test. But keeping him here would have given him the needed information to confirm who we are. And if he is Poneros, that would have been bad."

"How many more do you have?" Andreas yelled over to Clara after they had been quiet for a few minutes.

Madly searching, they examined box after box. Clara could feel her arms growing fatigued, but she felt exhilarated by the action. She had spent so much time studying, reading and talking that now action felt great. "I have seven more. How about you?"

"I think four more. It's not here. We have to get moving. Where's the next cargo hold?"

They both wrapped up the loose ends, scanning the remaining boxes. Clara showed Andreas the blueprint of the airport projected on her tablet. "This other hold should be readying packages to go onto planes in the next hour. If it isn't there, it is already on the plane. If we don't find it in the next twenty minutes, we are too late."

The door slammed behind them echoing the heavy beat of Clara's heart. She inhaled deeply, but stopped just short of letting it out when she saw the baggage handler leading Jahida inside. Her face was already bleeding, and he twisted her arm until Clara heard the snap of bone. The silence that came from her lips was almost as excruciating as the fracture.

CHAPTER THIRTY-ONE

"*E*lpis, have you seen Andreas? I thought we could spar a little before dinner."

Elpis looked up from the screens, not registering the question. His eyes were hazy from not blinking as he scanned the intel as quickly as it poured in from several outside locations, as well as from Heathrow. He didn't have time for interruptions.

"Are they on a mission?" Tom wheeled an extra chair around and lowered himself slowly, as he took in the images before him. "Heathrow?"

"Yes. We're having trouble locating the explosives. I really thought that last cargo hold was it. Where are they? We're running out of time." Elpis ran his hands through his dark hair, speaking more to himself than to Tom. His eyes scanned the screens. But he found no solace in the images before him.

"Where have you checked?"

Elpis slid the blueprints from his tablet to the screen above so they could both look at them. He pointed to two areas marked in red. "There is one more hold to check, then the contents are being loaded. Once they hit Chicago, we will be too late. We have to find them here."

As they looked up to the screen, they saw the same image. The camera was far from the individuals in the massive room, but the angle revealed what was happening.

Elpis shot from his chair. Assuming he was solving yet another problem, Tom continued to work from his seat long after Elpis had gone.

"How dare you use that to come here!" Eleanora's graceful fingers pointed to the tunic in Elpis's fingers as the venom poured from her lips.

"I thought it was fitting." His tone remained calm...and then it escalated. But the panic in his gaze betrayed his voice. "We were in France. Do you remember? 1194, I think it was. Jump in because my memory occasionally gets hazy after all this time. I believe I used it to save you from... well, you know. The Athoos thought this sacred cloth worn by Mary during the birth of Christ was lost in that fire. But they found it three days later, just where I had left it with you. But, the past, as you so often remind me, shall remain." His bitter tone dragged behind him, a cloak concealing his clashing sentiments.

"What do you want, Elpis?" She pulled her long blond waves over her right shoulder, exposing her left. He couldn't help but look. The beauty that remained was tainted by the years they had spent at odds, but it remained, nonetheless. A cynical goddess, she stood before him, directing her team of Poneros, just as he directed the Go'El.

She was a traitor. He needed to remind himself of that.

"You need to get them out of there. Now!" His eyes rested on the screen she held, and the earpiece she absently stroked.

"And if I don't?" she responded coldly.

"If you don't, Eleanora, he will kill for her. He will kill them all."

Elpis turned quickly, tunic in hand, and left her again.

He didn't see her eyes widen with fear. He missed the emotion sweeping across her skin. But he needed to get back. He couldn't let Andreas make the same mistakes that he had made. Elpis had to learn from his malignant choices.

Yet, it didn't stop him from remembering.

It had been thousands of years ago, a ridiculous amount of time when referencing one's memories, but, they were Elpis's memories nonetheless.

Eleanora, how can you protect him? They say he stood on that hill and watched while Rome burned. Why do you believe he is worth saving? Nero killed his mother, his step-brother...do you know about his wife? Remember the mission. Remember what we are here to do. Stop protecting him. Not everyone can be saved.

Elpis burned with the memories of a history long and arduous. It wasn't just her beauty that had drawn them together, it was her heart. It was the way she would insulate even those who were difficult to champion because of the cause. They had been there to stop Nero, the corrupt Emperor of Rome. Their Go'El mission was to eliminate his threat to Christianity.

Nero was burning Christians in his garden as a source of light.

Her dulcet tones had rolled over him. He was a slave to her voice, to her very presence. *Elpis, Nero's mother was a power hungry extremist who positioned him where he is today. Without her presence in his life, he would never have become what he did. I don't defend what he's done to the Christians, nor do I defend his treatment of the Jews. But I do believe that love makes you better. It makes you stronger. So I ask you, Elpis, what would our lives be like without love?* Her eyes had turned their intensity on one of the many busts of the Emperor that lined the corridors in which they traveled.

Elpis had fallen in love with her long before that day. But it was that evening, when they had infiltrated Nero's walls, freeing Christians and Jews in their wake. That was when Nero had snuck up behind them in a corridor beneath the Domus Aurea. Elpis could do nothing but watch as Nero drew a dagger down Eleanora's chest. The wound was deep and blood poured from her heart.

Elpis rushed to her first, immediately trying to close the source, but could see nothing except the blood. In seconds his anguish turned to malice. His generous heart solidified as he yanked the dagger from the hands of their attacker, who stood smiling at his kill, and swiftly slit Nero's throat. History would write that the emperor had cowardly taken his own life.

Eleanora was gone to him, or so Elpis thought. But he carried her body to the surface, taking in deep gulps of air as he prayed for her survival.

He never saw it coming. A mallet, Elpis thought, had slammed into his skull as he emerged from the tunnels. Later he would hear about the chaos that ensued because of the death of the emperor. In turn, Rome and modern civilization were plunged into the Dark Ages. But Elpis knew history was drawn that way because a Go'El had given in to his darker side and taken the life of a Poneros.

In his mind, he had lost Eleanora that day, though the truth of that moment had remained a mystery to him. It wasn't until centuries later that he learned he had been wrong. The Eleanora that Elpis had loved never emerged from those tunnels.

CHAPTER THIRTY-TWO

*T*he blonde-haired devil held a fistful of Clara's hair and yanked hard before she could react, and her body was dragged away from Andreas as if she were a ragdoll. Hearing the crack of her kneecaps slamming upon the cement, Andreas was blind with rage. All training engaged, his fist pounded the face of a second aggressor. As quickly as his nose snapped, his opponent's fingers released Clara from their vice, leaving her panting for breath. Taking a moment to see that Clara was all right, he returned to the fray.

Clara pounded the ground with a fist, forcing her strength to return. Lifting herself from a crouched position, she heard the sound of metal meeting flesh. She watched as Andreas slaughtered the life from her attacker. Clara's vision blurred with tears of fear and pain. She had never seen Andreas fight with such rage. If he delivered one more blow to the head of the first Poneros, he may never get up again. As his hand rose for what could have been the final onslaught, Clara saw a knife slide cleanly into Andreas's back. The attacker, however, could not depart as stealthily as he had approached.

The need to protect Andreas pushed Clara into action. She heaved her aching body across the floor with all the strength she could gather. Sliding toward Andreas, her hand dipped inside his boot, removing the silver switchblade. Wildly, she drew the blade behind the knees of the second Poneros before he could make his move.

A scream like he had never heard forced Andreas to break from combat. Looking at his own fists now covered in blood, he spun his neck in search of Clara. He found her huddled beneath him like a lioness protecting her cub. He yanked her into his arms and strode the length of the complex. Confirming their safety, Andreas secured them as far from their original position as possible. As quickly as they had entered, the Poneros had disappeared. All that was left in their wake was the body of a friend, Jahida.

CHAPTER THIRTY-THREE

Clara tore off her jacket and tossed it to Andreas. "Hold this against Jahida's chest."

His reaction was not to question but to follow her instruction.

"It looks like a pneumothorax; some studies say holding a soft pillow against the chest wall will splint the fracture." Clara didn't look up from her screen as she communicated with both Andreas and Elpis. "I need a laser. Elpis, can you get one to me?" Clara couldn't remove herself from the ground of the last cargo hold, but she began searching furiously.

Andreas held the coat to Jahida. "Can I tape this to her, so I can help you?" he asked.

"No!" Clara barked in response. She was completely in control. "She has a collapsed lung because a broken rib has pierced it. If you tape the ribs or chest wall, it can impair her breathing and she could get worse. I need her stable until I..." her voice faded as she waited for Elpis's uncharacteristically slow response.

Jahida was unconscious now. Andreas effortlessly lifted a substantial box and positioned it so that it held the coat to her body. Then he moved beside Clara to see what she was doing. As she waited for a reply, she leaned over to x-ray the wound on Andreas's back. Seeing that it was a clean cut and finding comfort in its steady healing, she returned to her work.

Not looking up, she gestured for him to go to Jahida. "I read an article about a team in Israel headed by an ex-general of the Israeli army." Clara said. "They have a patent pending that will change the face of airport security. These explosives made it through even the newest security upgrades. And why are the Poneros targeting cargo planes and not passenger jets? Airports can only scan little more than half of the packages that are being shipped via cargo planes. It's a calculated risk. So why would they target these types of planes? Anyway, these guys from Israel invented a device that uses Raman Spectroscopy..."

Before she could finish, Andreas cut her off. "Seriously? This is what you were thinking about?"

"Turn Jahida on the side of her broken rib. I know that's odd, but it will allow her to take deeper breaths. The rib is already healing; we need to ensure it stays out of harm's way. If the lung doesn't inflate on its own, I'm going to need you to do it."

He looked at her incredulously.

"You are all right. I'm all right. Jahida's alive. But we are on a clock here." She pleaded with him; a look he could not fight.

"What more can I do?"

"Well, basically, these Israeli scientists shoot a laser at a package like the one we are looking for, and through predisposed algorithms in their computer, they are able to read whether the electrons send off the right 'signature' to allow them to identify an explosive."

"That was dumbed down?"

Elpis interrupted, "I can't get a laser to you in time. Is that truly our only hope?" His voice sounded relieved even amidst the chaos that existed.

Clara pulled her eyebrows together in frustration. "They shoot the laser at the box and it tells them if the device is there. If we had one, we might be able to find the energy signature. There are too many boxes for us to continue searching one by one." But as she spoke the words, she only then realized what she'd said. "I can see energy waves. At least I can see their patterns. Most of the time, I don't know what I am looking for since everything has a different kind of pattern?"

"What does that mean?"

"Sometimes, if an extreme level of energy is being emitted from an object, I can see it. I can see refractions of colors that are not explainable through what people refer to as visible light. For example, if people can see Roy G. Biv as visible light, I can see Roy's next door neighbor UV light and Gamma rays...but only if they are excited. It's kind of like the new airport security scanners where people hold up their arms. Human energy is already moving and excited. If I can find the patterns of excitability that I'm looking for, I should be able to see it without the laser. I may be able to see which package has the explosives. It would contrast with the objects surrounding it and should stand out."

"Your strengths grow daily now, don't they?" Andreas stared at her in wonder.

Clara soaked in the compliment as she calibrated energy levels.

"Hate to interrupt, but we are on a serious deadline," Elpis reprimanded as he skimmed Clara's data.

"Hold on..." Clara knew there wasn't much time for analysis, but there was even less time for mistakes. They had only minutes before more Poneros could ascend upon them or Athoos would demand answers of them, and the last thing they needed was media in here when the airport was seething with Poneros.

Andreas began to pace. He walked over to the storm of boxes. What if she couldn't see the energy emissions? She didn't have time to calculate the algorithms and reprogram her computer to display the patterns. The cargo loaders were going to be here in five minutes and would need to start loading the packages onto planes. They needed more time.

"I've got it!" Clara declared. "This is what it should look like." Clara pointed to the array of patterns on her screen then swept over to the boxes in full stride. Her head traveled back and forth like an old-fashioned typewriter, scanning each row as quickly as she could. As she did, she could hear Andreas talking.

"Elpis, be ready to get us out of here. We don't know how unstable this bomb is or if there is a remote detonator. Let's get it away from the masses and dismantle it on our own turf."

Clara silently agreed, biting her lip in frustration as no energy source was seen. She began to worry that she might not be able to see the electromagnetic waves after all. Silently, she ran down ways to remove Andreas from the room so that she could deal with this on her own. He didn't need to be a part of her failure. She turned back to Andreas and pointed to the right side. "I'm not seeing it here. Let's try the other side," she directed.

Clara's turbulent movements forced him into motion before he even realized what he was doing. She was already digging into a pile of boxes by the time she stood beside him. "Do you see something?" he asked.

"It's here!" she pointed to an area filled with ten or twenty packages. "It's hard to tell which package it is in the pile. Scan these; hurry!"

Clara was already reaching for a package before Andreas could gauge how to help. The box looked identical to those beside it. Andreas gazed at his tablet, confirming that a printer was inside.

Goose bumps stood like soldiers as she saw a cellphone on the image in front of her. "Elpis, get us out! There is a remote detonator in here."

They raced to Jahida, taking out the Ankh and footprint, while never moving their eyes away from the sinister object in their hands.

CHAPTER THIRTY-FOUR

No longer in the sweltering garage, Clara focused on the room in which she now found herself. Mahogany tables warmed the well-lit room. She sank to the floor needing to find purchase in something solid as the adrenaline from her ordeal began to dissipate. Her eyes took notice of the craftsmanship of the intricate carvings that were wrapped around the legs of the tables. On one leg, Icarus flew, wax wings melting in his assent, too close to the sun, not heeding his father's warning. Another leg revealed Narcissus enraptured by his own reflection. Each carving, each myth a warning about human flaws apparent in every civilization since the dawn of time.

She looked down at her hand and noticed her fingers intertwined with a man's. Andreas searched her face but did not move his fingers. They trailed up to the pulse on her wrist, as if ascertaining her survival. Clara gently removed her arm from the silent embrace and squeezed the package that her other hand pressed tightly to her chest. Cautious, trying not to jostle it too much, she wondered how long it would be before the Poneros sought retribution through the remote detonation.

Tom was at her side instantly, although she had seen him sitting by the screens at the far end of the room only seconds ago. He pulled the package from her clutches and imperceptibly laid it on an empty table. Opening the top slowly, he asked, "What will I be looking at?"

Clara got to her feet and pushed toward the table. The adrenaline of the last few hours had dissipated with the acquisition of the explosive. She realized only now that the throbbing in her knees matched the metronome of her heart. And her scalp burned from the abrupt pulling of hair it had endured. Her first inclination was to redirect white blood cells to her head. By doing so, she quickened the healing process with a simple thought.

She cleared her mind before responding, "It's inside the printer cartridge" Clara watched as Tom delicately removed the printer from its box. Andreas appeared at his side, lifting the cell phone from the brown cardboard. After situating Jahida in the medical facility, Elpis returned to carry the explosive into his adjacent lab for study and isolation.

Clara opened the printer top to reveal the cartridge holder. She flattened her lips in concentration as she placed the tiny offender on the desk. Using needle nose pliers, she pried the exterior cap off the cartridge. Peeking inside, she saw nothing amiss. In fact, she was struck so deeply by the utter perfection of the device that her heart plummeted for a split second with the possibility that they had been wrong.

No explosives in the printer.

But then she saw it. Tucked neatly behind the ink packets, was enough PETN to blow a hole in the side of a plane. Looking up at her counterparts she explained, "Pentaerythritol tetranitrate. It seems to be the bomb of choice these days." Her shoulders settled in the realization that she hadn't been wrong.

"What do you mean?" Tom asked.

"PETN is a white powder that's been around since

World War I. It's similar to nitroglycerin but is seventy percent more powerful than T.N.T. It's much more stable than nitro and it doesn't explode when it's dropped or set on fire. It must be detonated"

"Are you saying that this is not going to explode right here on this table?" Andreas had positioned himself so close to her that it seemed they were now breathing as one. In fact, it felt as if he was trying to push himself between her and the explosive.

"I don't think so."

Andreas raised an eyebrow.

"Not unless someone within the vicinity is able to detonate it. I think we are probably in the clear. She lifted the box and turned it in her hands, examining its every nuance.

Andreas circled around to the cell phone detonator and held it up. His eyes squinted not in strain, but in concentration.

"The box was addressed to a Jewish community center in Chicago. Do you think that's just coincidence?" Clara placed the box back on the table with care. She looked up at Andreas, who held the detonator, and then turned back to the box.

"Let's just disable it and *then* have this conversation, shall we?" said Tom.

Andreas was already prying open the back of the cell phone, exposing its circuit board. Clara used tweezers to pull the wires from inside the tiny vessel. Both moved with accuracy and precision, as if they were dancing familiar steps. With a final flourish, they each used scissors, much like those used to cut cuticles, in order to sever the connection between the wire and the device.

CHAPTER THIRTY-FIVE

"*T*oday, for my current event, I would like to share some news about a little known occurrence from last week. Two bombs were discovered at two separate airports. They were both hidden in printer cartridges placed inside printers that were being shipped to Chicago. No one was injured because inside sources were able to dismantle the two weapons, and they don't believe there are more." Tara stood at the front of the class projecting an image of a news article from the *Chicago Tribune* on the Smart Board. She paused, looking at her peers and teacher for acknowledgment.

"And why do you believe this story is significant?" Elaina asked her student, as she always did. She was constantly trying to force them past the point of simply regurgitating information. Teaching, to Elaina, meant extracting the unique interpretations that lay dormant in the minds and hearts of these teenagers and, in turn, coming to their own conclusions. It wasn't memorizing facts or reiterating discoveries made by others that constituted a great thinker. It was discovering things for oneself and feeling the sense of accomplishment in the discovery. "Did anyone else read a different article about this event? Were there any details or perspectives we can add to it?" Elaina stood to the side of the classroom. Twelve years into her teaching career, she still loved every minute of it. It gave her solace when her grandmother had passed and it allowed balance between being a mother and wife and a person with a sort of secret identity.

"I heard about another article. I don't remember which newspaper it came from, but my dad was telling me about it. They think that the people who may have been involved in this attempted bombing may be the same people who were reportedly inside the military base for that shooting that happened a while back. Remember? Unknown people came in, stopped the shooter and then disappeared. Now they are saying that maybe the same people were seen on airport security feeds. A cargo hold operator claims to have talked to them. He is saying that they really are the same people from the military shooting. Some grainy pictures are surfacing from there, too." Saad spoke fast as he relayed the information to the class.

"Why would that be significant?" Elaina asked once again, struggling not to engage in the conversation herself, but move it forward.

Saad was pensive for a moment, "Well, it would be a big deal if there was some rogue group who isn't sanctioned by the government coming in and saving the day. I mean, people can't just go around and take the law into their own hands. We have a process. We have a system in place so that no one person can determine the fate of others." Saad smirked in response to his interpretation. He sat back down and crossed his arms over his chest.

"I think it's great! Why can't we live in a world where good people do good things without asking for anything in return?" Muhammad stared at Saad.

"Look what I just found..." Tara drew their attention back to the Smart Board, where unbeknownst to the others, she had been searching for a more astute answer to her teacher's question. "Check this out."

Another Faith Shaker

Here we are again, just months after my last report and more "crop circles" are appearing. How many more questions will be raised before we begin to demand some answers? Reports from an anonymous source tell this journalist that the now infamously thwarted bomb plot planned for an air cargo plane was actually halted by two of the same individuals who were responsible for the disarming of the suspected military base shooter.

That's not all my source told me...

There are vague reports indicating that at least one of these individuals had been in fact shot, but neither deaths, nor hospitalizations have been recorded. Similarly, these individuals were seen by an airport worker during the second event, but disappeared from a cargo hold before any further security follow-ups could be made.

There are two implications here and as a reporter, I am bound by integrity. If these individuals are vigilantes, taking the law into their own hands, they are also defying the very marrow of this country. If not, if they are super-powered individuals created by our government to dominate other world forces, there is no limit to the secrets that this administration is keeping.

Regardless, we are at an impasse and the need for answers is a loud scream from the mountain tops.

And so I ask: If you are the individuals or you have any information regarding them, please contact me through the information included below. We cannot put our faith into something that we cannot see.

CHAPTER THIRTY-SIX

*"T*his is their new tactic." Clara slammed the paper down on the table in front of Elpis. "I should have seen it coming. I knew they had something up their sleeves."

"Are you referring to the Poneros?" Elpis's eyes scanned the dark words popping from the gray paper. He still preferred this old way of reading to the tablets, though he had conceded years ago that information came so much faster via this new technology.

"Yes, the Poneros," Clara snapped, her anger toward herself escalating in the understanding that she was brought here to anticipate these kinds of events.

"What are you thinking? What is their plan?" Elpis had to curb the amount of questions that were piling into his head as he traced a hard line between the words on the paper and the look on Clara's face. "Are you concerned that people will believe this kind of thinking? Who would?"

"My family..."

"Do you remember them?"

"Does it matter?" Clara volleyed back, fury surfacing in her eyes. She knew that his question was more about the process, since she was the first of her kind. She understood that on some level she was still an experiment to Elpis and normally it didn't bother her, but today that question rubbed her raw. And in moments like these, it wore away at her that she couldn't simply find out more about herself. Protect those who remembered her love. It would be so easy. But Elpis had taken that option from her, and she couldn't help but resent him right now. It was that irrational thinking that rendered her motionless in thought.

She knew that this anger was what the Poneros had been hoping to evoke. At their core, the Poneros's goal has always been to divide. The more that humans and Go'El alike could resist that tendency to turn on each other, the more they could tip the scales back in their favor. Clara craned her neck in an irritated stretch and allowed the blood to calm and her breathing to normalize.

"No, of course, that isn't the point." Elpis pulled back, calming his own spinning mind. He reached out to touch Clara's shoulder, an offensive move to quiet her electric nerves. He had to remember that she hadn't transitioned all that long ago and the emotions of that progression were still in turmoil. He'd had his memories, and as they were torturing him as of late, they could also be a comfort to him. He saw the same in Andreas and in Tom, as well as others.

But with Clara he couldn't empathize, which only made her feel more isolated.

"Elpis, they are trying a new strategy and it is a gamble, but without understanding their game plan, we are flying blind. They are calling our very existence out into the open and challenging us to come forward. They are denouncing the very existence of God in a way that most Athoos wouldn't notice directly, but may begin to question internally. Questions like these belong in the tabloids, but these questions come from credible reporters. Incredibly editorialized, but presented as credible. That seems to be the strategy of most news organizations these days. Unfortunately, the evolution of news today has become acceptable in that fashion. People want affirmation of their beliefs. It's why there are openly left or right wing news channels dedicated solely to their cause of choice. And it's why their numbers of followers are so high. Some people even claim they are expounding on unbiased news because they are so satisfied with the fact that someone on television is confirming their beliefs."

"What does this have to do with the article?" Elpis continued to scan the words looking for insight into any connection to the Poneros.

"It has everything to do with this article." Clara spread her arms wide in exasperation. "The Poneros couldn't have played this card one hundred years ago. Heck, they couldn't have played it twenty years ago. But people are primed for these kinds of stories."

"Keep going."

"For one thing, news travels at the speed of your fingertips, from one person to the ears and eyes of hundreds of thousands in a matter of milliseconds. This article, although you are looking at it in hard print, has not only reached the fingertips of those few still reading paper, but it already has had one million hits on the web and it was only released today. It is trending on twitter and eighty-eight thousand people have liked it on Facebook. It doesn't matter who he is or why he wrote it...he is getting airtime and that's all he needs. The seeds of doubt and insecurity that the Poneros classically prey upon have been dispersed and I don't think this is the end of it. Like pistols at dawn, they are going to try to draw us out, and it will do one of two things. People will crucify us for our differences, once they see them. Or their faith in whatever they have held close in those dark hours will be stripped from them. The world and God or gods that they knew and trusted will burn and the civilization just might go down with it."

Elpis tapped his fingers in a silent drum against the table as Clara expounded on her thoughts. His reactions were minimal. Outwardly, he took the same shallow breaths in and out that were characteristic of his serenity, but inwardly, the storm was beginning to crash down upon him. Here he stood, looking at this new recruit. Unique in every way, she epitomized all that they believed to be good in this world, but now her very existence may tear them down.

"I told them that we couldn't increase the numbers. I told them that if we allowed any of you to be identified, we risked our own annihilation."

"It isn't about our existence. It is about the world. Talk about the tipping point. Think about the examples of religious persecution and their effects on the world. The Poneros have been behind every life altering religious movement that has ended in lives lost and massive division. We are at the precipice of another." Clara snatched her tablet and revealed a picture. "Today, people are still being persecuted for their beliefs. The news has no interest in what is really happening, and since no first world country will take a moral stand against the killing, the cycle of persecution continues. The history books whitewash events, and the cultivated ignorance is what turns people against one another. It is a pattern that we cannot ignore. The Communist Party of China has banned the practice Falun Gong, which is a philosophy based on moral viewpoints, truthfulness, compassion and forbearance. The Party declared the practice heretical. That was in 1999.

"Look at Martin Luther. Most people celebrate his view that a person's salvation could not be bought, but rather was a gift from God. He translated the Bible into Latin and today Lutherans still follow his belief system. But he was also anti-Semitic. Three major religions were in contrast during that dark time. Stalin was teaching Atheism in schools in order to make his ideal communist society.

And Bloody Mary was burning people at the stake for following beliefs outside the Roman Catholic Church's doctrine."

"There is no argument that the history of faith is a bloody one." Elpis flipped the screen with one finger as Clara presented him with a new example. He fought for his composure, maintaining clarity by what she put in front of him, but he couldn't help but wonder what Eleanora's role would be in all of this. To Clara, these time periods were lists on a page, moments recorded for posterity, but Elpis had been there. And Eleanora had been at his side. Now he had to think that she was at the helm of the latest deceit. Had she been the one to extricate the Poneros from the airport? Or had they conceded in defeat?

"Imagine, Elpis, if it wasn't just one religion against another. Or one political philosophy against another. Today, the fracturing of groups is limited to pockets. These conflicts are expressed through civil wars, criminal violence, political instability, or territorialism. This is enough to make people doubt that peace is an attainable concept. But what if our very existence fed into all of the insecurities of each faithful individual on the planet? Oh, they would persecute us. I have no doubt of that. But if they could prove, even for a second, that we are all individuals who have died, only to be resurrected for some sort of religious war, then that would create a global divide the likes of which we have never seen. The poisons of existence would consume them, and they would lose hope.

"The global impact of the Crusades and World War Two were the greatest we had ever seen. Still, that was only two percent of a much smaller world population. Combine the increased population with a communication network that allows every individual to be on the front lines and to alter the ethical code that has been a constant since the dawn of existence. The Poneros will tip the scales because the insecure and fearful outnumber the faithful. And within them is where the Poneros will fester."

CHAPTER THIRTY-SEVEN

She couldn't stop her fingers from dialing the number, even though she could hear Tommy shouting in her head. *You need to move forward, Mom. Go to work!* "Yeah, Mark, I still have this bug. I won't be coming in again today. I'd hate to get any of you sick." The sour taste of her lie swam through her mouth.

Adira lay in her bed, dark covers pulled over her body, shutting out light, noise, and scent—every sensation that could possibly remind her of him. The problem was that she shut the emotions inside.

He was with her, no matter how hard she tried to push him out. And the worst part about it was all she could see were the wires, the blue veins, the still lips, and the white pallor of his skin. All she could see was death.

And it had taken her child.

Days of severe depression seemed to come less frequently as time progressed, but when it came, it blasted her back like an unexpected wave against rocks. She could not stand. She couldn't breathe. And she just wanted it to consume her. Tearing the covers from her chilled body, she twisted her feet and placed them on the floor. A slow rise took her to the covered window like a small vessel ascending on the tide. Her delicate hands pulled the shades to the side, only enough for one eye to peer out to the courtyard.

The sky was a turbulent display of gray ranging from light to dark. All the trees stood vulnerable, leaves spread beneath them as a sacrifice to winter. Before turning back to her sanctuary, Adira caught a sight of the last golden yellow leaf hanging precariously from the tree above. As suddenly as she laid her gaze upon it, the rebel broke free, spinning and twisting with the wind. The golden goddess danced her last, a ballet of slow then sudden movement as she swayed toward her final resting place below.

Her eyes began to dry in the trance of the conductor-like movements, and Adira was startled when she heard a pounding. The steady thump, thump, thump was louder and stiffer than the pumping of her heart trying to fight away her sorrow.

Then she heard it again. It wasn't a soft knock, either. It was one of desperation and determination.

Holding the curtains with white-tipped fingers, she didn't move in an effort to argue with her subconscious. *If I don't move, whoever it is will go away.*

"Adira, open up! I know you're there. I saw your car outside."

She felt the blood rush from her face. It wasn't a fast drop; it was a slow torture that usually only comes before vomiting. It is that moment when every sensor in your body warns you about coming torture. Moisture races at top speed around your dry mouth only as a tease, not a fulfillment. Chills dance along your arms, back and neck. The knees you thought were a support, give way. And your eyes fill with unwanted tears. It's as if your body can do nothing but attempt to purge all the poison that has seeped into your atmosphere.

Adira took the moment to absorb the information and the visceral reaction that came with hearing her ex-husband's voice. She looked for a weapon. Something that would make her feel less vulnerable than the last time she had seen Adrian. She vowed on that day that he would never hurt them again.

How did he find me, she asked herself? She'd been covering her tracks for years. And she had become damn good at it.

"I have known where you were for the last couple of years. I didn't want to..." he hesitated, seemed to be searching for the right word... "hurt you anymore. I've tried to change. I just want to talk to you. Damn it, Adira, I'm in the hallway."

Adira pulled her feet over the side of the green comforter, snatching a pen from her bedside table and tucking it inside the band of her watch under her baggy sweatshirt. She wasn't stupid. But she was too nice for her own good. She knew she shouldn't be opening the door. Her hand froze a few inches from the metal handle and she clenched her shaking fist.

"When he knew he was dying, Tommy sent me a letter. He said he forgave me. He said he had to for himself and for you." Adira heard Adrian's voice crack with emotion. She hadn't heard that sound since the year they had met.

She felt her fingers wrap around the cool metal before she resigned herself to opening the door. With her other hand, she twisted the bolt and thought she heard an exhalation of breath on the other side. It was ever so faint; it may have been her own.

Adira pulled the door toward her inch by inch, expecting a torrent of anger that always seemed to come with Adrian. But he waited politely for her to ask him in, and didn't even try to reach a limb through the crack.

Her thoughts seesawed as she took in his appearance. He was still beautiful, in that edgy, dark sort of way. She'd always likened him to a fallen angel with his bright green eyes and long eyelashes that never seemed to fit with his square jawline and hardened features. Adira's eyes traveled down his body, seeing the familiar peak of dark hair whispering under his V-neck shirt. His leather coat was open, his jeans hung low and baggy; even though that was no longer in fashion, he made it his style. And his boots, still perfectly polished, rested on top of one another as he leaned against the door frame in anticipation of Adira's decision.

"Do I really need to stand out here while I'm talking to you?" His smug smile elicited all the emotions that Adira had fought so long to push away.

"Yes, you do. You are lucky I'm not calling the cops on you right now, Adrian." Adira could feel the heat creeping up her neck as the fury of the past consumed her again. He was the only person on the planet that could make her feel this way.

His lips curved up into a suggestion of a smile, as if he not only expected that response, but wanted it. "I deserve that." He brought his hands up and pulled away from the door frame. Searching Adira's eyes, he could see a stalemate, so he pushed his fingers into the back pocket of his jeans and returned with a square-folded note pressed between his second and third fingers. Reaching toward her, he held it out, conscious not to pierce the threshold.

"Is that it?" Adira's hands itched to take it, but her self-defense classes had taught her nothing if not to keep her guard up. She kept her left foot poised at the edge of the door so that it wouldn't be easy for him to push his way into the room.

He looked down at her foot as if to acknowledge that he knew exactly what she was doing.

"Toss it in the room. I'm shutting the door to read it. You can stay out there or leave." She was proud of her strength. It had taken a long time to get to a point where she could unflinchingly respond in such a way.

Allowing his smile to widen, he flicked the paper toward her couch with the grace of a longtime smoker, then again lifted his hands in a show of submission. He took a step backward.

Adira slammed the door with a suction-like sound and quickly flicked the lock into place. She leaned her hands on the door as adrenaline continued to course through her. She took deep breaths as she realized what had just happened. She thought about asking if he was still there but honestly didn't care. She felt a sense of triumph with that thought as she took steps toward the paper.

Sitting on the floor next to the small square, Adira prepared herself for Tommy's words. Not only were these the words of a child who'd been taken from her, but they were words that could potentially make Adira regret decisions that she had made in Tommy's best interest. What if he hadn't understood and never told her? What if he had wanted his father in his life and felt like she had been keeping them apart?

What if?...

Such debilitating thoughts are what cripple you in mourning. Adira remembered standing in the receiving line for a classmate who had died in a tragic drunk driving accident. She hadn't known him that well. It was more that she knew his friends and had seen his smile. She had seen the light in his eyes. And maybe there had been a part of her that needed to see that the light had gone out in order to believe it.

Standing in that line, she couldn't help but avert her gaze from the mangled body that lay open for view in front of the long room. His parents had wanted an open casket for the other seventeen-year-olds to see what comes of bad decisions. A lesson to us all, she had thought. But in that moment she wasn't quite sure of the lesson. The mortician had done her best, but the bruises weren't concealed. She averted her eyes as best she could. The sympathy cards along with the flowers were Adira's only redemption.

We are so sorry for your loss.
—The School of Business.

What if he'd finished college?

Please accept our condolences in this difficult time.
—The Everetts.

What if he'd married Suzanne Everett?

The 'what ifs' of a frozen timeline.

Those cards were what debilitated Adira at Tommy's funeral, too. It was what they said and what they hadn't said. It was the list of what ifs that accumulated as the day went on, and at the top of that list was, *What if your father had been here?*

"Why didn't you come to the hospital?" Adira spoke loudly through her mist of thoughts.

"Did you read the letter?"

"No, I haven't. Do you have somewhere to go?" She knew she shouldn't be engaging with him, but she couldn't help it. The anger for what he'd put her through surfaced like the head of a rattlesnake and danced within her. He made her love him and leave her family. He'd hurt her until she was bloodied and bruised, and every breath she took was a reminder of that suffering. He had hurt Tommy. When Tommy had tried to stop Adrian from dropping his final blow, Adira had braced herself, pulling her limbs into a tiny ball. Instead of the impact she had expected to feel, she heard the crack of breaking bones and skin against skin. The crack had not been hers.

That was the last of it. She couldn't take anymore, so when they left the hospital that night, they left Adrian for good. Pressing charges seemed futile, but in hindsight Adira had wished she'd left some sort of mark on Adrian's record. But she'd wanted a clean break. No deposition. No paperwork. No trial. Thankfully, she had revitalized her relationship with her mother, but going to her would be too obvious. Together she and Tommy had survived.

And then he got sick.

Adira's eyes drifted away from the door and back to the folded note that lay upon her floor. Tommy had left the trail. She reached over and held it in her hand. Smoothing it with the tips of her fingers, she searched for any trace of her little boy. She held it to her nose, but pulled it away violently as she smelled the sweet and sickening scent of the tobacco she knew Adrian chewed.

Adira took a deep breath and slowly unfolded the note, careful not to disturb its peaceful slumber. The moment she saw his six-year-old handwriting, she felt the tears spill over her cheeks. Ignoring the torrent of emotion, she scanned the words in front of her for any resentment toward her. She didn't think she could handle that today, maybe not ever.

Dere dad

 Im riting two yu in the houspitel cuz I now im gonna dye.

 I don't want yu to come here cuz I don't want yu anywear nere my mom.

 You don't deserv her cuz she is good and yu are not. but I am riting cuz yu shood now that I fergiv yu for being stupid. Yu mad a lot of mistakes but I am not won of them. I don't want mom to ever regret having me or being with yu to get me.

 The to of us together were something yu couldn't understand becus it was beautiful. And now I am leaving her alone.

 So. I fergive yu cause I beleeve that to get to where I want to go. I have to be better than you.

 And I am.

   Tommy

 PS-Don't come to my funral eether.

Adira couldn't wipe her tears away fast enough. Her chest ached with the emotion of love for her child and hatred for a world that had taken him from her.

"I can hear you crying. Just let me in. Adira, I promise. I am not going to hurt you. I am hurting too. I am pissed off. I am pissed that this great kid is gone and that I never got to really know him. I am pissed that I let my anger and my drinking take over. I'm sorry I hurt you. I'm sorry I hurt you both."

There was that crack again, barely audible through Adira's short gasps for calm. She was so tired. She was so tired of fighting alone, of crying alone, of being alone.

Pulling her worthless body from the floor, she padded over to the door and slowly opened it one more time. Adrian's face was taut as the light from her room slid over his skin. She opened the door enough so that he could slide inside.

CHAPTER THIRTY-EIGHT

"*W*ould you go to dinner with me?"

Clara looked up with a fog of incomprehension over her eyes from hours of reading and watching various screens of information, not to mention the physical and emotional turmoil that had been her last forty-eight hours. "What?" It was more of an exhale than a question and sounded more abrupt than she had intended.

"I would like you to take a break from this and go to dinner with me." Andreas's smile underscored his invitation.

She had read descriptions of men by authors that characterized smiles as lopsided, but there was nothing lopsided about Andreas. His smile was wide and true and sent a wave of emotion over her, forcing her to smile along with him. The sensation wasn't mesmerizing as much as it was like a relief.

Over the past weeks the awareness that she felt when near him was a constant yet welcome distraction. Clara's guilt over feeling anything that took away from the mission at hand was becoming debilitating. Her conflicting emotions were beginning to wear on her and she had no one with whom to discuss such things.

And that worked as a constant reminder of her role and cultivated within her a sense of urgency to accomplish something she wasn't sure was attainable. Could she really do what she had been brought here to do?

Both she and Andreas had spent many hours with Tom, as well as with Banko. Tom's innocence and incessant need to please others tugged at her in an intensely maternal way. She knew he did the same with Andreas. He, however, had felt a kinship to Tom, probably seeing much of his younger self in him. They spent hours together, almost like a family, pulling Banko into the mix as well. Her intelligence had always been intriguing to Clara, but it was the way in which she unfalteringly made decisions and never looked back, that fascinated her. Clara envied the young woman and found herself studying her thoughts and moves. Together, they were a daunting force. However, in those moments it left Clara feeling empty of an ability to make decisions based on experience.

Then there was Elpis. Andreas and Clara spent the most time with him. Though it seemed it was always work, they often spent leisure time together too, philosophizing and speculating long into the evening. Clara couldn't help but feel that even after all this time Elpis was holding back. He gave so much of himself; it was impossible to ignore that. But Clara couldn't shake the feeling that something was missing. Clara felt worn from just a few months with the Go'El.. How could Elpis have held on for so long? There had to be something tethering him to the cause. What was it?

"I can't go to dinner, I—" Her delayed response faded with her conviction.

"The balance can wait. And I can help you sift through..." He looked around the piles of research that surrounded Clara and waved his hand..."whatever it is that you are focused on, tomorrow." He didn't want to push her, but there was a little boy in him whose excitement couldn't be contained.

Having a personal life outside of the Go'El missions was accepted; in fact, it was encouraged. She looked back at the work that lay ahead and took a deep breath. "Okay. I mean, I have to eat, don't I?"

"Tell me what your life is like outside the missions," Clara prompted hours later. "I've read the reports and your files. I know all that you have accomplished, but I know nothing of what your life is like outside what we do. I mean, do you often have dinner like this?"

"Is that your roundabout way of asking me if I have dated anyone else?" Andreas tilted his head to the side, his dark waves sliding slightly with his posture.

"I didn't ask—" she stuttered trying to find the right words. Instead, she took another bite of the lobster in front of her. She doused it in butter and lemon sauce and raised it to her lips. "I have never tasted anything like this before. I mean, not that I can remember. And reading about it in books is not the same as tasting it." Her tongue darted out of the corner of her mouth to catch some butter that drizzled toward her chin.

"The people here go out all the time. I mean, you can't go through what we do and not need to blow off steam when you are off mission. It is easier to stay among our own; it allows us to be ourselves in a way that is impossible with Athoos, although we can cultivate friendships with them. And some do." His voice faded at the thought and Clara could see it was clearly painful for him.

"I know. I mean, I read about it in your file," she said quietly, not wanting to assume she understood the pain of his loss. "I'm so sorry. That must have been...difficult." She struggled with finding stasis between logical responses and emotional ones. They didn't come naturally to her new self, but she was working on it.

"Yes, it was," he clipped. "Friendship can't be based on a lie." He didn't want this dinner to be about his loss. "But

I have never been on a date with anyone...here for as long as...well, as long as I have been here." His smile turned almost triumphant, yet still timid. "I have been waiting...for the right person."

His coy response caught her off guard. He turned his chin and looked up at her as if he were hiding something.

Clara's flush resurfaced and she looked down at her food once again. "I have no idea if I'm waiting or not," she quipped. And he laughed, relieving some of the tension that lay between them.

"Is it hard, not having memories of your other life? I mean, maybe that's a stupid question, but help me understand what it's like." His body unconsciously slid toward her in anticipation. The rules were very specific. He could not tell her anything that he knew of her former life. Her mind had been so delicately rewired; Elpis wasn't sure what kind of emotional strain she could handle on top of the influx of information that she was experiencing daily.

Andreas worried about Clara because people that maintained a high level of intellect so often struggled with relationships in a way most couldn't quite understand. It was difficult for them not to follow every detail of conversation and interaction. If the Poneros posed questions, it was easy for them to exploit insecurities, fears and sadness. Everyone has them. Everyone feels them. But, people have to maintain the equity of those emotions. If the Poneros could tilt the delicate balance, then the person would sometimes topple into the darker world.

Those were the people who became Poneros and served to accomplish their mission in the same way that Clara and Andreas had been recruited to do the opposite. The problem was that the Poneros could infiltrate directly into the human world because those emotions were ever present and sometimes easy to manipulate in weaker individuals.

The Go'El had been chosen to manage those emotional weaknesses through superior strength and

goodness. Clara had been brought in because so many of those intelligent people had turned to the Poneros for camaraderie in their darkest moments. Nothing is more comforting than knowing that you aren't alone in your thinking.

Clara still hadn't answered his question. She was alone in her situation and he wanted—no he needed—to make an attempt to be a part of her world.

"I don't even know how to describe it. If it isn't in a book, then I don't understand it. I have read about childbirth, I have read about parenting techniques, I have even read about the feelings mothers have toward their children, but I don't understand what it's like to be a mother. There is a part of me that conceptually weighs out the high probability that I was a mother on the other side, and just as likely to have been a grandmother. So not only do I have no memories of those experiences, which is excruciating enough, but I also lack any emotional association to them. And it is beginning to eat away at me. I don't understand love. It's because of this gap in experience that I question my effectiveness." Clara's eyes drifted away, distancing herself from Andreas.

He placed his fingertips on her skin, softly brushing her hand, and watched the goose bumps rise on her arms, racing toward her neck. She jerked her eyes back to him, widening them in reaction. "You understand love. You are capable of feeling it. And I'll help you learn the rest." His gentle touch turned needy as he clasped her fingers to intensify their connection. She didn't recoil, and he thought that to be progress.

"What was your family like?" Clara's eyes met his but demurely jumped to his chest when she asked, "What was your wife like?" She pulled her hand away with those words and awkwardly took her napkin as if she had to wipe her mouth. It felt wrong, somehow, to maintain a physical connection with a man who had once loved another. It felt like she was exacerbating the deprivation in

some way, by gaining through another's loss.

Soon she felt her heartbeats even out with the lack of contact. This isn't why I'm here, she told herself. I can't get close to him. I can't feel these things. I must stay sharp.

Andreas leaned back in his chair and finished chewing the bite he'd taken to distract himself from the disappointment from Clara pulling away. He wiped his lips gently with his napkin, all the while watching Clara's eyes as she focused on his mouth and he on her. He smiled slightly at the attention, not new to him, even here, but he had never cared until now. He craved it from her. "My wife was my great love." Stopping at those words, Andreas saw Clara's eyes swirl with conflicting emotions. He saw a flicker of jealousy, combined with that of intrigue for a qualified understanding of this emotion to which she was so drawn.

"I loved her from the moment I laid eyes on her. We saw the world together, and I can't even imagine having really seen anything without her by my side. It's funny." He paused for a moment, putting his hands on the table. "You talk about love and I think about all of Elpis's theories on balance. But love is the greatest imbalance. Because, Clara, it threw me right out of control, and I am not sure I ever recovered. People talk about the antithesis of love being either hate or apathy, but I believe love might just be the only experience in the universe that doesn't have a definable opposite."

"What do you mean?"

"Well, you need pain to understand the lack of pain. But there isn't an opposite emotion to love; there is just its absence. Because when you are in love, you can't imagine the world existing when you didn't have it." Andreas stopped for a minute and realized that he was heaving undefinable emotions at Clara which she couldn't understand. "I'm sorry. I know it's a feeble description. I know that there is nothing more annoying than hearing someone say that you can't understand something until

you experience it. That used to infuriate me, too. And I am not doing much to help you understand love. But this excitement that I feel when talking about my other life...I haven't felt it since...since, I was an Athoos. Now I am feeling it again." Andreas let his words hang between them, and for once it appeared that Clara was a step behind, taking in his words, instead of being twelve steps ahead of him.

Her hazel-oak eyes struck him with their storms of sentiment, always clashing with her thoughts and research. Like a planet, he couldn't see her constant movement, but he knew it was there, never ceasing.

"Tell me about your children. What was it like to be a parent?"

"As a guy you don't really think about it much. I mean, it's a distant thought. I knew that it would happen someday, but I wasn't built for it and consumed by it like she was." Andreas waited for a look of recognition or understanding from Clara. Her eyes darted to her food once again and he knew that she had understood the reference. "Even when she was pregnant, I wasn't sure how I would feel about it. I was a Greek man born of a generation that left it to the women to rear the children." He waited for Clara to understand his meaning with a grin on his face. "I know, rather obtuse in comparison with today's standards, but true nonetheless. She would call me on it, too. She never said it like she was nagging me; it was like a snap of a towel, pushing me back to reality. Even though she had her cultural standard bred deeply within her to make me happy, she knew I was just as responsible for her happiness. And every time I took a drink, I stole a piece of that from her." Andreas's face grew serious with that admission. But it was an admission he needed to make.

His eyes drew together in what Clara conceived to be a memory invading his consciousness. She wondered silently what it was like to attribute a memory to every spoken word. She hated that her words were connected to references, like footnotes in a research papers. They didn't breathe and ache the same way that Andreas's did.

"She would put me to bed, like a child, when I drank too much. And each time it happened, I vowed it was the last time. Like every addict, I made promises to myself and to her that I couldn't keep. And every time I couldn't keep them, I knew that she felt like I didn't love her enough to change. I hated myself for that. I hated that I could never convince her that that wasn't the case. I'm not sure that I ever did." The pain in his expression was evident. "But when we had our first daughter, it began to click. Weaknesses are a failure, but they are not a sentence. I will never forget standing in that hospital room looking at the miracle that we had created. We loved each other enough to conceive a little person who could potentially make a difference in the world. And outside of fighting in the Navy, I hadn't made a difference at all. The insanity of war is something that no training program can prepare you for. Outside of the Go'El simulating facility, nothing can prime people for the emotional strain of watching women, children, and brothers suffer. I couldn't get those images out of my head. I know how weak that sounds, and how useless it is to lay blame anywhere but within yourself. But, at the time, it was why I started drinking. It didn't take much." He smiled, a slightly cynical laugh escaping with the thought. "I was never this big in my other life, and even with all the drinking, I never really built up a tolerance either. So, I chose to turn numb. I chose to turn it off and it was easy and cowardly. But I did it."

"Post-traumatic stress disorder is seen in one in eight..."

He laughed, interrupting her train of thought. "Clara, you don't need to quote percentages of PTSD for me. I'm trying to make up for those mistakes. I can look at myself in the mirror again. I had to. Because when I held that little baby, a piece of me and a piece of her, I had to change. I guess I just needed to know that I could. When she was pregnant with our second, I remember thinking to myself that it would be impossible to love all of my girls. But your heart makes room. I became the man she needed me to be; the man I wanted to become. And then I got sick..." Andreas left it at that. He skimmed his fingers over the hair on the back of his neck and leaned back in his chair, lost in thought but returning to Clara every few seconds.

"What was her name?" Clara asked.

Andreas blinked, out of reverie or out of surprise, she wasn't sure. But he didn't answer for some time. He looked down at the table, straightening the fork and knife that lay on his plate. With his initial movement he could have sworn his finger passed through the fork, but when the utensil moved as he'd originally intended, he focused again on his next words. Then his gaze returned to hers. "I can't say." He smiled, though it didn't quite reach his eyes. "You know the rules." He slid his hand over hers again. "You know how Elpis is with the rules."

CHAPTER THIRTY-NINE

"We got a call in from Detroit. Are you in?" Tom asked Banko as he grabbed his duffel bag from his room and began sorting out laundry from the basket to fold and place inside. Though he could not specifically define why, he felt a little off balance.

Banko sat with her feet up on the coffee table; her laundry had been folded and placed in her basket, ready to transfer back to her apartment. On her tablet the contents of the same report that he had just received was open.

"This guy is a vet? Are we sure about the intel? How has he not been on our radar before this?" She swept her finger from page to page and used her thumb and forefinger to enlarge the uploaded snapshot of the target. Then she minimized his picture and began reading his bio. "The target has had at least six incidents that should have landed him in prison. How is he out? I mean, he armed himself with bombs thirty years ago and took his psychologist hostage. Look at this." She pointed to the screen, her thumb running over her bottom lip in a nervous gesture to which Tom had grown accustomed. "He took his nine-year-old son and a gun, rented his own plane, tried to land at LAX so that he could hijack another plane to take him to Iran. These don't even include the threats he made to Carter, Bush, and the Veteran Affairs offices. How have we missed this guy? Why hasn't the news reported on any of this? There are no references in anything public. These records are sealed, and only the Go'El have access to them." Banko's agitation had increased so that she rose and was pacing the floor.

"Who could be so devious as to seal records, persuade probably traumatized, if not PTSD-affected individuals to revolt against the institution of government because of the atrocities that he or she saw during Vietnam?" Tom exaggeratingly tapped his left index finger against his temple.

"I know, but even after this amount of time, the Poneros still get to me." He knew how she felt. It was what pushed Tom to accept the next mission. He needed to be in the fight. Because if he wasn't...

He thought back to all that he'd been through. He and Andreas had shared a sandwich between sparring matches and spoke of the families they'd left behind. It had felt good to peel apart the depths of emotions that had debilitated him, especially after his last simulation.

"What do you remember about being sick?" Andreas had asked him. He didn't pin Tom with a look, but patiently waited for the painful flood of memories.

"Looking back now, those thoughts are hazy masses of tormenting moments. I remember it all. And I remember nothing." Tom wrapped the remnants of his sandwich and tossed it into the can next to the bench. "I don't really want to remember. I just want to move forward and make all that suffering worthwhile. Because when I force myself to remember, all I can see is my mother's face. It tormented her because she couldn't save me. Now, I need to save her."

The fog of the memory dispersed and shook Tom back to reality. He turned to Banko and voiced, "So, get your bag. Let's do this one together."

"This is where the satellite tracked his plates last, but there's a delay. The bartender said he was making threats to the Islamic Center of America. Didn't he claim to be a convert to Islam around the time of the crazy Iran hijack attempt? This guy is straight up nuts." Tom's unwavering eyes traced the horizon, hoping that they would find their target in time.

"It doesn't take sanity to be part of the Poneros posse. Some of the time, and I'm guessing this may be one of them, it isn't even a Poneros who's acting in their favor. Plant a couple of them in a bar with an already riled up, inebriated vet who has the propensity to tilt the wrong way and boom, you got yourselves a ready-made disciple to do your bidding with no investment in training needed. Pun intended, by the way." Banko's hands gripped the steering wheel, keeping her foot to the floor as they sped past sign after sign, aching to make time.

As they made their way past the last checkpoint, he caught her profile. He had always respected her and they had instantly become friends. But now, he noticed the calm beauty that surrounded her. The inky silk that stopped at her shoulders framed delicate features that belied the strength that rested in Banko's mind and body.

"I hate to interrupt," Clara cut in, and both Tom and Banko drew their fingers to their earpieces, "but I just spoke with the Director at the Islamic Center. I explained to him that we were working on a tip and that alerting anyone at this time may be the wrong move, but he is more than concerned. He has five hundred worshippers in there right now. It would take some time to evacuate them and I don't want to do that unless we know there is a credible threat. What are you seeing?"

"We are almost at the location. We'll keep you posted." Banko tightened her grip on the wheel and shifted in her seat.

"Please hurry." Clara's tone echoed in their earpieces and Tom swept his feet together, prepared to move.

Banko had made the call to be transferred to the bar location with a vehicle to track the target. Now she was regretting the decision not to go directly to the Islamic Center. They'd thought they would have more time to intercept. Now they realized their error, and five hundred lives were on the line. "Tommy, doesn't this thing move any faster than this?"

"I didn't pick the car. And you're the one driving."

She pushed the pedal to the floor and counted on her quick reflexes to get them out of potential danger. Their eyes flashed from side to side, scanning for any clue that they were on the right track. Tom's eyes caught a glimpse of a single shoe by the curb. On his many trips to the hospital with his mother, he had always wondered where the random objects belonged that had been abandoned alongside the road. His mother had once told him that all those objects had their own story. Today he found himself aching for his mother and wondering about the story behind that abandoned shoe.

Clara chimed in again before he could think of the part of his mother's story that he was missing. "He is armed with M-80s." She was quiet but resolute. Knowing this was as close to a confirmation as they were likely to get that this was no longer a non-credible threat, all three remained silent for a time. If they alerted the target, he could go early. Now, they just needed to stop him.

Flying onto the curb in front of the Center, Tom was out of the car before Banko could turn off the engine. They both spotted the car at the same time, just as the target opened the door.

"Sir, I'm going to ask that you turn around and place your hands on the roof of the car, please." Banko had already pointed her weapon, and in the darkness Tom could see the faint green dot placed above the knee. She was making the choice to drop him or to bleed him out. The femoral artery was not far from the knee cap. He knew the mental calculations she was making. They were trained to limit death. But sometimes that meant making a choice that some would find impossible. If she didn't eliminate the target, there was a possibility that even with a severe injury, he could detonate explosives or fire a weapon. Both of these options could mean lives lost.

The target stared at her, an Asian woman standing before a good ole boy who'd fought in 'Nam'. Tom could only imagine the drunken thought process that was flowing through this guy's brain. He raised his weapon and took a step around the side of the car, revealing his form to their objective. From his stance, he could see no weapon, no strapped-on explosives. All he could see was a man who looked like he could have been his father. Flashes of the simulator infiltrated his brain and in the time that it took to push away his dark thoughts, the man raised a weapon that must have been hidden under his coat.

Banko didn't hesitate. She took the kneecap first, which dropped him to the ground. Then, with the ping of metal on metal, she shot the weapon from his hand, taking two fingers with it. Tom shook his head with disappointment in himself, and relief that his partner hadn't needed him.

Tom walked to the vehicle to ensure that the threat had been nullified. Banko found the keys inside the owner's pocket and tossed them to Tom. He cautiously opened the trunk. "Banko, take a look at this."

After cuffing the now unconscious target, she walked over to him. They both stared at the pile of M-80s and other materials that were stacked inside the trunk.

"Are those fireworks?" Tom asked as he picked up a box to study the contents more closely.

"Those are Class Cs. That's a fifteen-year felony in Michigan, not to mention possible charges for religious persecution." Banko slapped a hand on Tom's back as they peered inside the open trunk.

"That's a long sentence," said Tom.

CHAPTER FORTY

"*H*ave you heard about this?"

Muhammad referenced a link to a small article from a less than prominent news site. "I'm guessing by your silence that you haven't. Seriously, this is outrageous!"

"First, tell us about the article and then give us your claim about the media. Then we'll talk." Elaina tried to redirect her already emotionally flustered student.

Putting down the pen he hadn't realized he had been drumming nervously against the desk, Muhammad clicked on the link and waited while the article loaded onto the Smart Board. He scanned the class for looks of recognition and formulated his claim in his mind as he waited. He knew that saying 'my dad said...' would reduce his credibility for this discussion. However, after a lengthy conversation during dinner last night, Muhammad had found that what his dad said now became his own thinking as well.

Media Cover-up for Terror Plot Points Fingers at Religious Conspiracy

A former American soldier is in jail today after an attempted bombing of the largest Islamic site in the United States. The sixty-three-year-old man was arrested in the parking lot of the Islamic Center of America, while an estimated seven hundred people were inside the building. The man's car was filled with high end fireworks and M-80s, all of which would be considered viable and significant weaponry if used in a closed building. Thanks to the quick action of law enforcement, police followed the tips of a barkeeper who heard the bragging confession of the man over a whiskey.

Which leads to two pertinent questions...

First, why is this article the only source to report on an attempted bombing? Is it because the phobia against the Islamic community has become so widespread that when a white man attempts to target this particular group of people, it is not considered newsworthy? Or is it a stain on our country that a veteran would make this kind of heinous decision?

Secondly, why is it that the "police officials" who intervened yet again, were not police at all? Rumors are surfacing again indicating that the two individuals who vanished from the scene quickly after the suspect was detained were part of the undisclosed organization of vigilantes.

Will these "vigilantes" come forward and assuage the panic that their actions, though seemingly filled with good intentions, are causing?

Until then, it appears the questions will remain unanswered.

"People freak out when a crazy Muslim attempts to target a group of people, and rightly so." Muhammad's tone escalated with his last few words. "But the media does not help. This article is one of the few that even reported on the occurrence. How is this not headline-worthy news? It was a crime in progress in which over seven hundred lives were at stake. Reporters should report the news, not filter it. Don't censor it; just report it." He exited the screen which he had presented to the class and walked with sure steps back to his seat.

Elaina sat for a moment, and then asked, "Is Muhammad right? Do we live in a country where we have censored media coverage? Is this just one example of many?" Allowing time for the students to think of examples, she commented, "I am impressed with your ability to question journalistic integrity without making it personal, Muhammed, when clearly it is a personal topic for you. Keep it up; keep your sense of perspective."

Muhammad smiled at the affirmation and pulled out his notebook and a pen. He busied himself so the other students wouldn't see the pleasure that he took from his description.

Megan raised her hand and spoke at the same time: "I've heard that schools are more segregated today than they were in the fifties."

"I'd need evidence," said Elaina, "but I would imagine there is definitely a level of economic segregation, but maybe not as much racial profiling..." The students began to plug away on their laptops.

"This says that more soldiers committed suicide than were killed in battle last year," Chang yelled out.

"Really? Is it a credible source?"

"I don't recognize the site. It lists several censored news reports from each year."

"You'd have to cross-reference those kinds of claims with credible sites, which may be difficult if these are censored facts." Elaina never ceased to be impressed with the speed by which her students could attain information. "Why would information like this be censored?" Elaina pushed them to think further.

"If it makes the government look bad, then they would do everything in their power to prevent it from getting out. Faith in the government is a precarious balance." Eddie smiled because Elaina did.

"I like the way you are thinking today," she encouraged. "For tomorrow I want you to write a claim about something in which you have faith. And perhaps that faith might be blind," she suggested. "The claim can be religious, political, or personal. Think it through and provide evidence for what you write."

The groans always made Elaina laugh, but these were great kids. Sometimes they just needed to argue for sake of argument. Really, who didn't these days? She walked around the room picking up stray paper, pens and pushing in chairs as the kids shuffled out when the bell sounded.

CHAPTER FORTY-ONE

"We missed this because you were schmoozing with me at dinner!"

"I was not schmoozing with you. I am in love with you. And we didn't miss this because of the dinner. You are angry and it is interfering with your logical thought process, but you need to slow down for a moment. We missed this because we have no intel from Copenhagen. We have never, for as long as I have been here, had one mission near there. And none are on record since World War I. But, Clara, there just aren't enough of us. There definitely aren't enough of you to keep up with all the evil in the world. We can never stop all of it. It has to exist. As horrible as that is..." Andreas's voice drifted as he tried to dip his head to reach Clara's vision. She couldn't look at him. She wouldn't. And that was making it even worse.

"Andreas, thirty-eight people are dead. Two hundred fifteen are injured. How could we have missed this?"

"How do you know that it was the Poneros?"

"How could it not be? We can't fight what we don't know. And clearly, I am not helping!" Clara collapsed on the stairs of her apartment, pulling her knees to her head.

Her body shook with the emotions of failure and Andreas had no idea what to do.

Andreas lowered his powerful body beside her. He placed his coat around her shoulders in an effort to reduce her shaking, but he couldn't keep himself from touching her. Pulling her into the space between his arm and body, she folded into him without reservation. Andreas continued to hold her in silence for several minutes.

"It was 2004 for me," he began, speaking above her head as he rested his chin in her hair. Her face rested against his chest. "You may have read about it. It's still considered one of the worst attacks in history, although people weren't as aware in the United States. I didn't arrive until the second day." Andreas traced a stick on the pavement in random shapes as he spoke, his voice heavy with emotion. "I transported immediately, but communication at that time was still sluggish, so it took some time to get the information and be placed through the right channels to get anywhere near Ukraine. Close to two hundred children were held hostage along with one thousand others. A child watched as a gun was put to his father's head. Another parent was shot and dragged away to bleed to death. More were killed as one of the attackers dragged a group of men into an empty corridor and detonated a bomb. Others were executed in that same hallway.

"The Ukraine government was seething with Poneros, so there was no way that I could get close enough. We have no one inside their government and no relics to use as portals to those areas, so the transfer for me and my partner was difficult in itself, but getting any kind of credible information was nearly impossible. The second day was full of ridiculously posed negotiations that, looking back, I'm not sure were even happening. Ukraine was dragging its feet in doing what was necessary to save civilians, and it was confusing as to who was taking responsibility for the heinous crime.

"Honestly, to this day, I have nightmares about it. I was there and I have no idea what really happened. Who shot the first shot? Who set the explosives? In the end, I ran into the gymnasium filled with hostages so exhausted, overheated, and undernourished that they had taken off their clothes, drunk their own urine and didn't have the will to fight for their existences anymore.

"I couldn't save them all.

"I helped who I could, but knew I didn't have much time before the media would be there and governments would clash. Three hundred plus hostages were killed. One hundred sixty-six of them were children. It was the worst I had ever experienced, and I'm not sure I ever really got over it."

Andreas pressed his tongue to the back of his mouth and looked up in an effort to keep his emotions at bay. He hadn't talked about this in years and was surprised by how the memories had swallowed him.

They held each other in silence for what seemed like hours, but it was only moments. Andreas understood her vulnerability and Clara, his strength. Both needed something from the other. No words could replace that connection.

CHAPTER FORTY-TWO

"What are you writing?"

Adrian ran his hand slowly up Adira's spine as she lay on the other end of the bed. Before his fingertips reached her shoulders, a destination for which she was deeply longing, he snatched the pad of paper from beneath her.

"Don't read it. It's not done." Adira felt her hackles rise at his intrusion. She had been enjoying their time together, and blissfully pretending their history did not exist.

He respected her words enough not to look at the paper in his lap. He waited for permission.

In her weakness the night before, she had taken him in like the stray puppy she had fallen for so many years ago. She told herself this was different. She told herself not to kiss him, when he leaned toward her, pausing just centimeters from her, waiting for permission that she would give him too easily.

The kiss was just as if it was their first all over again. She moved forward feeling the warmth of his lips as they gently opened and closed, his tongue exploring hers. His kiss made her weak. She was helpless to stop it. The ache spread throughout her limbs and she knew she was powerless to push him away even if her mind was screaming at her to do so.

He knew too predictably how to please her, his fingertips brushing down the sides of her body, pressing into her back and inching her toward the bed.

She might be careless, but she wasn't stupid.

"We can't do this." Her voice was raspy with lust, but firm in signal.

She remembered how easily intense emotions could blur for him. Passion and anger could become bedfellows if she didn't react the way that he expected.

She took a step backward, almost expecting a blow. When it didn't come, she eyed him warily. Her shoulders felt tense, and her body was still humming. His eyes opened slowly and she saw his pupils shrink as his expression softened. It was in that moment that she made the decision to let him stay.

The next morning they found themselves entwined in another faceoff, Adrian holding her writing hostage and Adira wanting desperately to have it back.

"You know I like to put music to it. It's just lyrics and to tell you the truth, I haven't written or played since before..." her voice faded with sorrow, her eyes downcast and depleted.

"You can say it." Adrian's voice softened, as if making a plea. She wondered if he needed to hear her say it, in order for it to be true. She wondered if she could say it. Her body felt a piercing ache every time the reality of her world penetrated her mind. Adira fought hard to keep the poisonous thoughts from feeding her melancholy. But that kind of pain was impossible to control.

"You know what I meant."

Adrian was resigned to her answer and maybe to her need to hold those words within her. Still, he did not read the crisp piece of paper in his hands. And she did not ask him to. Tenderly reaching her fingers out to him, she turned her palm to the ceiling and waited.

He placed the paper back in her hands and exhaled a noisy breath of petulant disappointment.

She gave in and read it to him.

Betrayal

Stormy skies descend on the island of hope
Children learn, children play, children trust
Where is the god that understands the full scope
Of people's needs, people's wants, people's lust?
A single man took away the promise of their future
Someday teachers, someday cops, someday leaders
Where was the god who protects and is their watcher?
Never lover, never brother, never pleader.

CHAPTER FORTY-THREE

"*H*e set off a car bomb in the government quarter in Copenhagen first? How did we not get the call sooner?"

Clara sat at the desk, her green satin summer dress angled with awkward wrinkles because of her sidewalk cry. She was running her hands up and down her exposed arms. She felt the absence of Andreas.

"I'm not sure. We haven't been focused there for years and don't have any people directly involved in their government, so we must remain dependent upon communication between the government and police. We use the same channels any media source does for those interactions, which means our upload of information returns to a snail's pace. We are already trying to get someone in, as we speak." Elpis pulled the tablet from Clara's hands, since she had grabbed it from him as he explained.

"It's too late," she whispered more to herself than to the others. Shoulders slumped, all she could do was read the reports. The reports had been written as protocol after the event.

"These were mostly kids."

"Yes. Eight of them were in the government building..." His voice trailed off, the implication of who the remaining numbers represented was screaming between them. Elpis raised his hands to his forehead, massaging the area. Clara could see him pushing on his temples, but no indentations were being made in his skin. He'd been at this for hours, trying to recalibrate the locations of various Go'El in order to better address the needs of victims. He couldn't exactly call this a mistake, but he was having a hard time saying otherwise out loud.

Why were the Poneros targeting children? Yes, it had happened in the past, but this seemed so deliberate, so calculated. It was so close in nature to their attack in Michigan.

"Are they confirmed Poneros?" Clara's face flew to Elpis. The desperation transformed to hope.

"Yes, they have claimed responsibility." Elpis waited a moment before returning to his work. "Clara, you did not come here to thwart every incursion, but you *will* stop many of them. And that is what matters."

A rebellious tear slipped down her cheek with his words. But what frightened her even more than this atrocity was the realization that she wasn't certain how much longer she could do this. A part of her wanted to walk away and simply be with Andreas. That felt right. But he was now in Denmark.

They had sat for some time, holding one another as shields against their personal demons. She hadn't missed his words: *I'm in love with you*. The words had swirled around her, testing her heart and soul. Did she love this man?

He spoke of his wife with such adoration. How could she hope to compare? With no memorable background, how would she even know love?

Her attention returned to the reports in her hand. She saw picture after picture of each massacred child. It would later be said that one in four Danes knew someone affected by the attacks.

Clara snapped her gaze on Elpis. She needed answers. "Why not aim to defeat the Poneros once and for all? Maybe we can eliminate the greatest evil in the world by removing them, along with ourselves. Maybe then humanity will have a chance at redemption."

CHAPTER FORTY-FOUR

"I don't know what happened."

"What do you mean?"

"I froze. I had the shot and I didn't take it. My hesitation could have meant your life, let alone the seven hundred innocents folded in prayer behind us."

Tom put his head in his hands, annoyed by both the situation and his intense emotional reaction to it. The simulation from the other day had had far too much impact on his current state. Was it interfering with his ability to complete missions? If not for Banko's expertise, they both might have been compromised.

She looked at him with intensity behind her gaze. Having never seen him like this before, it startled her. His normally steel resolve was shaken to a point where the man in front of her appeared to have crumbled, as if a child. It was then she fully realized that not so long ago he had been a child.

Although she had spent the last year around Go'El whose stories intermingled with tragedy and completion, she was never able to fully be at peace with the transformation that existed in their world. To an outsider, all of the Go'El looked like prime specimens of men and women. Their bodies were in peak physical condition. Most Go'El liked to flaunt their bodies, not in a narcissistic way, but as people who had suffered and decayed at the ends of their human existence, only to become something that they had never dreamed possible. They were simply amazed by their metamorphosis.

Banko, in turn, had come from a large family in Japan. Like many others in her country, her house consisted of her mother and father, four brothers, her grandmother and grandfather, as well as her great-grandmother. As a child in Japan, nothing seemed unusual about the crowd in her home constantly hovering in and out of each other's business. The population had so drastically changed that Japan was leading the world in life expectancy. Her grandmother, at ninety-seven, was already fourteen years past the average age of death. She was one of far too many being kept alive through a feeding tube that had been implanted into her stomach.

Her great-grandmother had been ailing for some time, dispersed between the physical ailments of such an age and the mental difficulties of dementia. Banko's mother and grandmother had brought her to the doctor for treatment only to find, upon their return to her room, that a feeding tube had been inserted into her stomach without their permission. They were both devastated.

Banko's father and other family members had been strong believers in allowing nature to prevail. Although technology had improved to the point of sustaining life much longer, they did not believe in altering the fate that nature had laid before them through such artificial means. Buddha said we "should learn the art of healing in order to help others and to liberate them from suffering." As a family, they believed that this kind of "healing" was simply prolonging that suffering. The once joyful family became bleak and docile.

It was during that time that Banko's stomach had

begun to give her problems. She ignored it often, not wanting to cause more worry than her family had already endured. But, at sixteen, the pain increased, her weight decreased and on a cloudy Wednesday morning, Banko knew something was very wrong. She felt intense and sharp pains, not unusual for her, but at more frequent intervals than at any time before. As her mouth filled with moisture, she ran to the bathroom early that morning and heaved the contents of her stomach into the toilet. She looked down to discover that the toilet was full of blood. Her body responded with intense shaking, and Banko crumbled to the floor in the bathroom, too weak to stand or flush away the evidence.

And that's how her father had found her.

He swiftly carried her to the car, muttering prayers in her ears. Her mother sobbed as she entered the car. They drove in silence.

Once they arrived at the hospital, explained all the necessary information, took all of the necessary tests, and waited all of the necessary time, they heard the words.

Adenocarcinoma.

Cancer.

Cancer of the stomach.

It was already very advanced, since she had ignored her symptoms for so long. Her parents didn't dare reprimand her; the defeat on their faces was reprimand enough. There were treatments. They opted for the gastrectomy where surgeons would remove most of Banko's stomach. But even with that, they found that it had spread further. She went through the chemo and radiation, as so many others do. In the end, Banko found peace in her Buddhist readings and felt she was able to simply let go. She couldn't put her family through any more grief, and four months to the day from that bloody Wednesday morning, Banko sputtered her last breath and faded away into her transformation.

Her mother took the Buddhist writings from Banko's

cooled hands. Turning the binding to read the page from which she had last read, she saw Buddha's Four Noble Truths. She only got through reading the first:

"Human life has a lot of suffering."

Banko's dark memory faded and she returned her thoughts to Tom. "You suffered so much in your short life. Those images are not easily dispersed. You cannot blame yourself for needing more time to find your meaning in that suffering."

CHAPTER FORTY-FIVE

"*I*t's beautiful. Unfinished, but beautiful."

"It's painful. You always said that all I wrote about was pain. I fixated on the pain." Adira eyed Adrian through her last statement and wondered how he would interpret it. He seemed to gloss over its potential insult. "You told me I loved the cry-in-your-soup-shit music and that I focused too much on the dark side." She folded the paper, harshly shoving it into her back pocket and slid from the bed.

"You did. You do. But the pain is real. I feel it too." Adrian closed his fingers around her wrist as she attempted to rise from the bed. Pulling her down, he closed his lips on hers again. The kiss quickly turned desperate. She was amazed he had held out as long as he had. Which is why she had let him stay. The old Adrian demanded what he wanted. He took it when it wasn't offered. When she admitted it to herself, there were times when she found that appealing. She was young and wanted someone to make decisions for her. Even now, older and wiser, but scarred more deeply, she knew there was a part of her that longed for the same thing. Sometimes there are points in a person's life where they can only take on so much without support. Relinquishing control can be intoxicating, and she longed to let someone else worry for her. The pain was beginning to consume her. And the anger that came with it was her focus because it forced her to feel.

She gently smacked Adrian's hand away from her own, as it was stiffly holding her to the bed, and connecting her to him. She pulled away and walked to the mirror, pushing the heels of her hands against her eyes. Adira rubbed her palms down her face, trying to pull away some of the weariness and focus on the dark reflection that stilled behind her. Was she allowing this to happen so that she could feel something?

He was beautiful. Like the snake in the garden, he waited for her. He wasn't pushing her, but she could feel the strings pulling.

What was she doing?

Tommy would be so disappointed.

But Tommy wasn't here. And no one else was, either. And her little boy wasn't coming back.

Leaning against the dresser, she faced Adrian. Words weren't needed as they studied each other, both trying to ascertain the other's true intentions. They'd always been like that—predator and prey dancing in a circle of both malevolence and sentiment.

Adrian rose, taking slow but expressive steps toward her. He placed his hands upon her shoulders, toying with the ends of her hair that lay upon her shoulders. "Let's go somewhere together. Let's get away from the memories that plague us here and experience something new." He dipped his stance slightly, as if trying to tug her eyes back into his soul, a place in which she had overstayed her welcome so long ago.

"Adrian..."

"Don't say no. Don't let our past determine our future. You know we can be together. You feel it, just as I do." Adrian placed her hand over his chest and pulled her to him. She held her hand decisively over his heart and felt the strong rhythmic measure.

"But..." This time she faded before he could stop her. She didn't know what to say or how she felt. She couldn't break from the haze of emotion that held her like a vice. Maybe this was the way out. Maybe this was life moving full circle.

Maybe we are meant to be together and all this with Tommy...maybe it wasn't for nothing.

The sparkle in Adrian's eyes returned and he stood only slightly straighter, a sign of recognition that she was submitting. The predator positions its prey into submission. It was subtle, but Adira had learned quickly how to read his body. A talent cultivated out of necessity for survival. "Let's go to New York. We always talked about going to Times Square and finding those vintage record stores so that you could find inspiration for your music."

"That was back when there were records. They probably don't even have those stores anymore."

"Well, I guess we will just have to go to find out.

"Sounds like a plausible research assignment."

"I do believe it is. It is really for the good of civilization."

Adira's smile returned as their exchange bounced from one side to the other. This was the man she had fallen in love with. She had forgotten. Love had created Tommy.

CHAPTER FORTY-SIX

*H*e'd lost her.

It was all Andreas could think about. They'd finally connected. They'd made that connection real and then he'd lost her.

He had to get her back.

"Clara, I..." he wasn't sure what he was going to say, but he was positive that she wasn't listening. Her shoulders were taut, as if the strain of that position had left her numb. Her jaw flexed with each gnash of her teeth. "Clara, what's wrong?"

"They are throwing down the gauntlet," she replied without looking up.

Andreas glided to her, automatically pressing his thumbs into her shoulders, hoping she would relax. She felt the tension radiating from every part of her body. He was relieved when she audibly let out a breath with his touch.

Catching his eyes, she spun her chair around to hand him the document she was studying.

Xcxsiolyuffsnbchenbchenbunsiowiofxmnulnly
wlocnchaqcnbchnqiayhyluncihmuhxcnqiofxaio
hhincwyx?siogusbuhyvyyhuvfyniguchnuchnbyb
oguhjijofuncihzilnbcmfiha,vonnbchambupywbu
hayx.xcxsiolyuffsnbchesioqylynbyihfsihy?xisioeh
iqqbunvlchamniaynbyluxcpcxyxjyijfygilyyumcfsn
buhiolguhcjofuncih?uwiggihyhygs.siowlyunyxnbu
nzilnbygiylzywnfs.nbuhesio.

"Clara, am I really supposed to..." Andreas's eyebrows were raised in confusion, looking to her for confirmation that his vision wasn't failing.

"I'm sorry," she said absently and shifted images in front of her. "I received this message earlier. And of course realized that I needed a cipher in order to decrypt it."

"A cipher? Like a code?" Andreas was trying to follow.

"A Caesar shift cipher is actually very common. They aren't terribly complex to decode, if you have the correct cipher. Julius Caesar himself used them— twenty-six for each letter in the alphabet. Basically, you line up to lines of the alphabet, one above the other. Then you shift the alphabet by one letter at a time. If you know how many times to shift it, then you can decrypt the code."

"So you knew how many times to shift?"

"No, of course not."

Andreas continued to wait, but his patience wore thin as her agitation grew. "Clara?"

"I ran through all of the possibilities. I can actually see them without even writing them down. It's intriguing, my intelligence continues to grow and manifest in ways that I didn't anticipate." She looked up at him finally. And he took her hand, trying to slow her thoughts. "I'm sorry."

"It's all right, but you need to remember that I

don't talk code."

She smiled as she returned to her explanation. "It didn't take me long to run through the code. It was only six shifts, but I ran all twenty-six to be sure." She spun her tablet around where she had been taking notes, explaining the cipher without a thought. "It is basically two alphabets lined up one on top of the other. The top alphabet is the English one as we know it. A, B, C all the way to Z. While the bottom alphabet is also English, only shifted so that it no longer starts with A. Each letter of the top alphabet corresponds with one on the bottom. So if the top begins with A, and the bottom shifts six times, then the top A now correlates with a bottom U. Because G is the sixth letter in the alphabet, it now lines up with an A on the bottom. Then all of the rest of the letters follow suit, just shifted. If G matches with A, then H has to match with B. And so on."

"So, did you translate it entirely?"

"Yes. Here it is. And, Andreas, this may have been challenging, but they wanted me to read it. I am sure of that. They know about me. Am I the only one?" Clara looked to him as she handed him the decrypted message.

Did you really think that you could start recruiting within two generations and it would go unnoticed? You may have been able to maintain the human population for this long, but things have changed. Did you really think you were the only one?

Do you know what brings together a divided people more easily than our manipulation? A common enemy.

You created that for them perfectly.

Thank you.

"Is it me? Is it me that gave it away? Did my family see me? Andreas, tell me. Did I do this?" Clara pleaded with her eyes for resolution, but her body had already resigned itself.

"It could be any of us. Elpis knew we were taking a gamble by increasing the numbers. Almost every one of the newest Go'El have living family members. It has been easy to work around it because most of them were elderly in their human form, so after transformation, the youthful appearance that they acquire makes them unrecognizable to the Athoos mind. Most individual consciousness can't register that kind of reality, and even if there is a spark of recognition, most people chalk it up to a coincidence of characteristics.

"I have memories from my human life of seeing people that I thought looked like people I had known or even family members. Until I was recruited, it never occurred to me that those people may have been...something special."

Andreas slid a stool next to Clara and pulled her as closely as he could without removing her from her chair. Placing his hands gently on her knees, he lifted one hand to her cheek. He brushed the pad of his thumb along her bottom lip, aching to kiss away her fears, but knowing that this wasn't the time. Instead he spoke: "Clara, we can't know everything."

"But..."

"I know. You care. I care. I love that you have your heart and soul in this, but you can't let it consume you. And I can't imagine how hard this is for you. It must have felt like it was all you had because the memories aren't there. But that's no longer true. You have me. I will be your memories, and we will make new ones together."

"How can you be so sure about everything? You lost your wife. You didn't get to know your grandchildren. You didn't get to do everything a person should be able to do. Doesn't that make you angry?"

"My wife and I took a trip once." He started the story as if it had lived on the tip of his tongue for an eternity. "I had just been diagnosed, and we both knew that treatment meant the end. We...I didn't want to go out that way. Not yet, anyway. We had always traveled to Europe, having had family there...in Greece, it was easy. But we wanted that trip to be special. We wanted it to be ours." As Andreas spoke, he felt Clara pull away, but he had to tell her this. "We flew to Seattle for a weekend; saw the city.... We rented a car and drove a few hours—we wanted to hike up Mt. Rainier. At over fourteen thousand feet, it is substantial. People train there to climb Everest. Everyone thought we were crazy for wanting to climb it. All my wife's friends thought I was making her take this journey with me at the end of mine.

"As we neared the mountain, the clouds were massive. We couldn't see anything. We had resigned ourselves to doing it, so in our minds we thought, even if we can't see anything, it will be worth the challenge of the climb.

"But just as we were about to reach our starting point, the clouds parted, and there it stood! The mountain had been right there in front of us and we hadn't even seen it!" Andreas paused for a moment, palpably remembering the view on that day.

The vivid emotions elicited by his memories became her own. She clung to them, making them as personal to her as they were to him. Clara felt herself blinking away the tears that she hadn't expected to form.

"Anyway, we started our hike, making the first seven thousand feet in a couple of hours. Halfway to the summit, we sat on an outcropping of rocks. We were above the cloud line. Beneath us were the puffy fiends that had hidden our challenge. Straight ahead were rows of peaks and valleys, the likes of which no picture or painting could ever portray. The air smelled crisp and clean—we couldn't help but close our eyes and inhale the moment. As an Athoos, I felt close to God. Unbeknownst to me, I was...

We had crossed over a glacier—Rainier has twenty-six of them, even in August—and she tapped my arm, not wanting to bring noise to the moment, and pointed to the waterfall beneath us. I turned to look at the summit, so close to where we sat, but knew that we were only halfway there.

It was enough."

Clara wiped away a tear.

"We ate as we talked about the girls. We talked about what she needed to do once I was gone. We cried.

"When we started our descent, she noticed something and stopped me. Pointing to a gorgeous magenta flower that had poked out through a rock, she said, "Now that's tough." And I laughed, because she *was that flower*. 'This is God,' she said. 'This is how I know He's all around us. There is beauty in this world, and it's full of purpose. It's a constant reminder of who we are and why we're here. If this kind of beauty lives here on Earth, imagine what must come next for us.'"

Clara loved him in this moment for sharing this story. And his memory became her own.

"Her faith became my faith, and I was able to let go."

"So, now you are trying to hand your faith to me..."

He brought her to his lap, moving her as if she were a house cat. Squeezing her to him, he guided her chin with a finger toward his mouth. The kiss began delicately, their lips transferring all their thoughts and emotions with tenderness. Andreas smiled. He wanted to *remember* every detail of her face.

"God won't take away our free will," he said. "Without it we would never be able to see the beauty on the mountaintop."

CHAPTER FORTY-SEVEN

"Mommy, why are we going to New York?"

Elaina gazed at her beautiful little girl and missed her grandmother. She had always wanted her to be a part of her children's lives. It was the little things that tugged at her emotions. She tried to cut the kids' pancakes the way that Υιαγιά had. She scratched their little heads and backs the same way, allowing them to curl around her the way she had with her grandmother. She taught them how to play solitaire and watched their faces brighten when they could accomplish a win. She spoke occasionally with random Greek words, trying to hold on to the small pieces of her grandmother that had long since disappeared. In those moments that she allowed herself to remember, Elaina felt closest to Υιαγιά Clara. And that was why she wanted to go to New York.

"I've only been there once and I was too young to know the difference. And a friend of Daddy's is getting married. So, we are all going to go. Plus, it was where my γιαγιά and παππούς went for their honeymoon." She swept her hands over the princess braids in her almost three-year-old's hair and straightened her skirt.

231

"What's a yummymoon? Is it like yummynade? Can I have some?" Her smile was piercing, all chapped, food layered lips and baby teeth. It made Elaina's heart ache every time.

"A honeymoon is kind of yummy, but not like lemonade," Elaina laughed. "Give me the kissy." Her daughter knew the request, and responded without question. She stepped into her mother's arms and pressed her lips hard to Elaina's for what felt like minutes. Eyes wide open, execution flawless, it never failed to make them both laugh. Elaina tickled her as she ran away.

"Mommy, is Γιαγιά Clara in heaven?" Elaina's son looked up from hanging Batman off the cliff to ask the question that seemed to be plaguing him more lately.

"I think so, Dre. What do you think?" Elaina walked over to her son and handed him his flip-top cup of milk and sat with him, tying Superman to the same rope to save his friend, then thought twice about it and had the red and blue figure fly in for a pickup.

"I think so, too. I think she's in heaven with Papou and they get to play together. Can I go to heaven to see them?" That question seemed ever-present lately and she wondered often what he was thinking. It was such a difficult tightrope to walk as a parent. Teach them about faith and death without scaring them, but also not enticing them. Teach them to be confident without making them conceited. Teach them to be kind to others, but also wary of strangers. These were fine lines.

"You will go to heaven someday and you will see them again. But not for a very long time. You have to live your whole life and make new memories to bring with you so you can tell them all about it. You have far too much adventure left here to go yet. Besides, Batman needs some saving here." They made whooshing and banging sounds setting up imaginary worlds and breaking them apart.

CHAPTER FORTY-EIGHT

Elpis sat with Clara, heads bent low over research as usual. Tom and Banko found them that way.

"I'm glad you both are here. Clara is working on determining the next target. We may need to lay low for a little while." He knew his words were left unfinished, but there was no easy way to say this and no real way to stop what was happening. The world was a different place than it had been, and for the first time Elpis felt like he was no longer evolving quickly enough. "This age of media and quickly disseminated information is working against us. I'm afraid of recognition. People do not react well to unpredictability. Finding out about us could break them. The most devout could be used."

"Slow down, Elpis. No one will recognize me. I was a child. I never looked like this." Tom gestured to himself, but held tightly to Banko's hand.

"I know...I know..." Elpis's doubt was evident in his every gesture. He doubted himself and his decisions. This could mean a crisis. Not only of faith, but in the existence of the Go'El and humans and all that he had worked to restore and achieve. And all that he had lost. If the

Poneros were changing their strategy to something so confrontational, it could mean a serious attack in the coming days.

"The Poneros posted this where they knew we would find it." Andreas interrupted trying to bring calm into the tension filled room. He was not used to seeing his friend so frenzied. "But they said nothing of importance. They spoke directly to us, but gave nothing away."

"They knew I would find it. They knew where I would be looking. That's the problem," Clara cut in, cognizant of keeping her voice gentle. Everyone was strung tightly, ready to shoot off into several different directions. She had to keep them centered. They had to stop this before it began. *Where would they make their next move? What would they want?*

"Clara, they haven't given any proof that they even know who we are. Right now it is just conjecture and idol threats. It could be a rogue Poneros who legitimately recognized one of us. We don't know. We don't know anything right now, so we also can't react too quickly. They want us to do just that. They are trying to unhinge us." Andreas studied his team as his words downplayed the reality of their situation. They were being called into the light which either meant a standoff with the Poneros on a global level, or a crisis of faith with the Athoos. Neither choice was workable.

"You're right. It is their MO to optimize on weaknesses and insecurities. The difference is that they do it to Athoos who are vulnerable either cognitively or emotionally. We are neither. So, that would be going against their normal pathways. There must be something that made this contact time sensitive. Why now? Why this way? Why so obvious?" Clara put a voice to her concerns.

"Has there ever been anything like this in the past? I mean, have they ever contacted us in any way?" Tom was plugging away on his tablet.

"They've been subtle," Clara said before Elpis could

respond. He stood behind the group, studying the information before him, but she couldn't help but notice a flinch at Tom's question. She looked to him as she spoke. "I mean, we have always been present during the big events in one way or another, but the real standoffs were the ones most Athoos don't know about. Still, they have changed the course of history. The Poneros have never contacted us so personally..." Her voice faded with the recognition that the possibility of loss was ever-present.

"Clara's right. You know the rules. We can't interfere with their faith or their fate. We must remain subtle. We can help the Athoos with indirect ideas, but we can't take away their ability to choose. We were involved in most facets of the World Wars, but those were Athoos conflicts, imbedded with Poneros ideals. They have always been the catalyst. I met up with one before we destroyed one of their heavy water supply facilities." Elpis's mind wandered back in time, attempting to use any information from their history to apply to this day. He kept his distance from that which could reveal his own story.

"What's a heavy water supply?" Tom asked, ready to type the words into his tablet.

"It's a necessary element in the production of a nuclear weapon. Most people don't know how close the Germans were to creating their own weapon of mass destruction, but Elpis and some other Go'El destroyed it before they could complete the project."

Clara envied all that Elpis had accomplished in his time. Most of the others hadn't studied his past as she had. Plus, she often got the feeling that Elpis was a missing piece to part of the puzzle she had been thrust toward. Clara could not justify the feeling that Elpis was holding out on her. There was something that had manacled him here for this long, but that information remained steadfastly out of her reach. Frankly, since she had been here, she hadn't had time to focus on much aside from her missions. Regardless, no one could doubt that he was a key contributor in the planning and execution of almost every pivotal mission in Go'El history.

"We never sanctioned the building of nuclear weapons. We aimed at stopping the Germans first; we would have liked to have stopped the Americans as well. But we couldn't see an end to Hitler's wrath. He was weak minded and vulnerable to a Poneros like Mengele."

"Dr. Mengele, the angel of death, was a Poneros?" Tom was trying to keep up with this rewritten history.

Elpis could only shake his head in agreement while Clara put words to the facts. "He was steering that crazy train. The experiments for which he's infamous drove the evolution of their Athoos recruits. Much like our Go'El have superior physical attributes, the Poneros are capable of untenable emotional manipulation. Harnessing both of those kinds of power would make them unstoppable."

Elpis tried hard not to think of Eleanora. But the raw pain that lanced across his chest was a living thing. The battle to push it back was one he often relinquished to remind himself of the path ahead. Though the others were pensive in the reflection of her story, Elpis saw Clara's narrowed brown eyes following his every response. Clearing her throat, she battled on. "And after the Americans defeated the Germans, Mengele fled to South America. Elpis was part of the mission where Mengele 'accidentally' drowned."

"I still regret that he couldn't pay for his crimes more publically. The things he did to the Athoos..." All were silenced by those gruesome thoughts.

"Anyway, we directly interacted with the Poneros at the plant where they were producing nuclear weapons. They knew who we were; we knew who they were. But it was conversation. It wasn't an indirect threat. It was simply that we so often fight them, but rarely do they speak to us." Clara tried again to bring the conversation back. After a minute's pause, she added another example. "The Go'El were also involved with stalling the process of finding a replacement emperor after Ogedei Khan died."

"Am I really supposed to know who that is?" Tom pleaded.

"Sorry, he was the son of Ghengis Khan. He died before he could approve the invasion of Western Europe. If he had, or had his successor quickly moved in and made that call, Austria would never have initiated the concept of capitalism and modern banking. The economy as we know it today wouldn't have been created."

"Okay. Definitely subtle. I like it." Tom gave Elpis a smack on the back. Elpis laughed audibly with the cracking sound that echoed with Tom's strength.

"The wobbly chair was my favorite, though. Nice job with that." Clara smiled brightly toward Elpis as they shared a private joke.

"Care to share with the class?" Andreas's voice remained a cavalier blanket over the truth of emotions he had forgotten were so acute.

"Oh, sorry," Clara acknowledged the others. "Elpis realized that the Poneros had several interactions with an anarchist who had publically denounced the president elect, FDR. Rather than take out the target or risk public recognition, they simply handicapped the already not so mentally (or physically) stable target. They replaced his chair with a wobbly one that in turn forced him to miss the shot when attempting to assassinate Roosevelt. Had he succeeded, the history of the twentieth century would not be as we know it today. Roosevelt dug the United States out of the Great Depression by creating the FDIC which allowed Americans to trust the banking system again. He set a minimum wage, established child labor laws, and led his country through the Second World War. Who knows what the world would be like had Elpis left him in a stable sitting position?"

"Well done, sir." Tom extended his hand just as Clara continued talking more to herself than to any of them.

"All of these were public settings. All pre-planned

events that would change the course of history. The blog post is new. Look at the words." She read it again out loud, but her words were focused more on finding a solution to a problem than eliciting a response from her crowd.

Did you really think that you could start recruiting within two generations and it would go unnoticed? You may have been able to maintain the human population for this long, but things have changed. Did you really think you were the only one?

Do you know what brings together a divided people more easily than our manipulation? A common enemy.

And you created that for them perfectly.

"'...go unnoticed'" she repeated. "What are they noticing that they wouldn't have before? Exposure? The Athoos live in a world of overexposure. They tweet about buying a cup of coffee and instantly people have a picture of where they are, who they're with, what they are drinking. He knows who we are because our faces are easy to recognize if we are the same people involved in multiple attacks that have been stopped."

"I've been involved in all but one of the last four missions. Banko has been in one." Tom gestured to Clara and Andreas, furrowing his eyebrows in thought. "You two have been in all of them."

"I don't think the number is important. It might not even be about any one of us. Rather, it is about what is already public." Clara plugged words so quickly into the main computer that none of their eyes had lifted from the keyboard before she was already spreading out tabs on the main screen. There were more than fifty high profile events occurring that weekend around the world. How could they narrow to just one? Their forces were limited in number and there was no way they could spread out that far.

"I keep seeing the plan. I know there is something in these words. It was stupid to post this. Maybe it was a rogue, maybe it was just an imbecile, but it's so cliché to give your enemy any kind of clue. '...a divided people'. What divides us more than anything today? It sounds like they are counting on that division. Optimization for their convoluted use. Even bragging about it." Clara flipped from tab to tab; her eyes scanned the information as it was revealed. The others struggled to keep up with her mainframe mind.

"Men and women...something sexist?" Andreas worked to clarify her thoughts.

"No, I've thought about it. Sexism isn't the root of conflict today like it was years ago." Clara responded before it seemed he was even finished with his thought.

Then Clara suddenly smiled. The electricity of her expression awakened Andreas from his studies; his connection to her unbreakable. "What?" he asked. "You found something. What is it?"

She pointed at the screen and whisked away all other tabs. Their eyes focused on the news story that projected in front of them. "We can't be any more splintered than by our religious beliefs. It's no longer Christians versus the world. It is every faction of monotheism and polytheism. It is that divide that will destroy us. Every war that is being fought, and each genocide that is committed...that is the underlying commonality. The Poneros have aggrandized public perception. And they will do it again. If the world finds out about us, it will shake their faith regardless of religious affinity. They will either destroy us or they will investigate us into abolishment. And if they have any understanding of our motives, they will know that it goes against our rules to change their faith or their fate. We can't let that happen. Look at this."

Her words lay heavily on their minds as they read the article on the screen:

Religious Organizations to Demonstrate in Times Square

Several of the world's leading religious organizations and leaders will meet at a head to head gathering of the minds. Although the demonstration is thought to be a friendly reminder of the differences between peoples and their beliefs, authorities worry that this kind of a demonstration could quickly turn violent.

'When you have this many strong-willed people in one place, all desperately proud of their beliefs, one wrong word could turn to fury and defensiveness,' says the New York City mayor.

Security has been increased in anticipation for this display of First Amendment rights, set to begin on May 1st and culminate three days later in the square. The anticipated crowd for this gathering is unprecedented, as it is already the highest tourist area in the city.

"They don't need to expose us. To expose us means to expose themselves. The Athoos mind isn't prepared to comprehend that. But if they can get a weapon through that security, then they could blame any one of those organizations and start a war. We have twenty-four hours to stop it."

Clara stood with those words and faced the team behind her. They were ready.

They had to be.

CHAPTER FORTY-NINE

"Mommy, why are all these people here? I can't see anything! Can you put me on your shoulders?"

Elaina looked down at her little boy and pulled on the feet of her daughter as she explained, "I have your sissy on my shoulders; could you ask your daddy?"

"Come here, Dre." Elaina's husband lifted the four-year-old easily onto his shoulders. "No crying if your feet fall asleep, though."

They walked through the sea of people, trying to take in the sights, but all they could see were bodies. Fighting their way through the crowd meant a constant stream of pivots and turns that kept their eyes from the bright lights of Times Square.

They'd had an amazing trip, Elaina thought to herself as she pushed her way along the crowded sidewalks. The wedding had been a beautiful celebration of both love and life, not the pomp and circumstance of some weddings. The couple that had exchanged vows was a union of two hardworking people; one a fellow a teacher, the other a businesswoman. They volunteered each year for an organization that raised money to cover the expenses for refugees who had been displaced from their war-torn homelands. With the money they help to raise, they buy welcome packages so that the families have all the basic necessities to move into the apartment provided by the company. That's how they'd met. Together they put sheets on beds and cleaned bathrooms for people they didn't know and who would feel lost in a country where the language was not their own, but who had moved because it meant safety for their families.

And the organization didn't just leave them to fend for themselves. One partner continued working with the family after they settled in by teaching them to drive, use computers, save their money, and find jobs, while the other partner taught them the language, how to read, to write, and how to get around in their new communities.

The wedding made Elaina miss her grandmother and think of them traveling to America for their honeymoon so many years ago. She often wondered what they were like before they had become sick. Her memories of her grandfather had faded; some days she had a hard time remembering him at all before his disease had become terminal.

Clara's illness had so consumed the family for the last ten years that it was often difficult to remember what a pillar of strength she had once been for them all. She had been the problem solver. Like the two women they had celebrated this weekend, she had been a light in the world and in Elaina's family. Her memories of Clara would keep that light gleaming.

Soon after Elaina's grandfather had died, her father and mother had separated. Newly imbedded in the angst that was her teenage years, Elaina had spent the afternoon crying to her grandmother.

"Γιαγιά, why? Why did papou have to die? Why did my parents ever marry?"

"Elaina!" Clara had snapped. "Don't ever question your parents' love for each other. They loved. You were made in that love." Elaina's head rested in her grandmother's lap while Clara's long nails drew small circles under the thick hair that lay upon her granddaughter's head.

"We will always ask why, Elaina. Sometimes things don't make sense, and most of the time it hurts." Clara smiled at her granddaughter, easing the sting of her earlier reprimand. "Κούκλα, love means taking risks. Your parents risked pain by falling in love and making a life together. But they had you and your brother, and I doubt very much that they regretted that risk. But now, they've grown apart, and they may not be able to find their way back."

"What about you and Papou?" Elaina longed for answers. "Do you regret it? You aren't that old. You don't deserve to be alone now." New tears rolled down Elaina's cheeks. The tears were for her, for her mother and father, and now for her grandparents. Clara's heart ached. Not for herself; she had been prepared. She'd known that it was coming and they had been on borrowed time for these last months.

"Papou is in a better place. He was suffering, in pain and living with regret for his bad decisions." Clara found herself choking on her words, throat clogging with emotion she'd thought long past.

"How do you know? How do you know he is in a better place?" Elaina's thirteen-year-old eyes pleaded for certainty in her very uncertain world.

"Because I believe..." Clara tapped on her chest, smiling down at her little doll. "Jesus said, 'Have you believed because you have seen me? Blessed are those who have not seen and yet have believed.'" Clara wiped Elaina's tears. She gently pushed the brown hair behind her ears and settled her hands on top of her head.

"Γιαγιά, how do you believe so strongly in something you can't see?" Elaina asked a question that Clara herself had pondered over the years. Still, she wasn't any more prepared to answer it now.

"Elaina, there is no good answer to that. You are smart

and so you will question. But sometimes the least likely answer is the one that means the most. Have faith that you will make good choices, but understand that some things are out of your hands." She kissed her granddaughter's temple and lay quietly in silence.

Just as that last thought left Elaina's mind, her daughter pulled her hair gently. Elaina looked up to see the image of her family reflected on the side of a building in Times Square. The lights bounced around them even in the fading sunlight, bringing their eyes from one advertisement to another. But in that one image, Elaina could see the eyes of her grandmother in her daughter and the complexion of her grandfather in her son. Reaching for her husband's hand, she knew she had all the answers she needed.

CHAPTER FIFTY

"*W*hy are we here? This is craziness!" Adira could barely keep up with Adrian as he charged through the crowd, limply holding the tips of her fingers. "Why are you pushing so hard to get closer? What happened to seeing the record stores? Where are you going?" she repeated as she tripped on a curb and knocked into an angry demonstrator.

"You have to see Times Square," Adrian repeated as he kept her from hitting the ground.

They'd spent the last three days commiserating. That was the only word for it. Feeding off of each other's emotions, they blasted themselves into an onslaught of sinister thoughts. Their wretched darkness festered in hearts that were meant to be apart.

"Do you have any idea how many wars and diseases have ravaged this town alone?" Adrian whispered. "People are always touting this city as a beacon of camaraderie, bringing all kinds of people together, but no one mentions what the bringing together of those people has done."

Adira felt hazy from all the negative talk. She had been bombarded with it from the moment they had left for

New York. Granted, they were joined together by a mutual defeatist attitude about life because of the death of their child, but Adrian was pushing that attitude into every corner of their experience.

"Yellow fever and Cholera ran rampant for hundreds of years, killing thousands of people." Adrian let the thought settle as he saw the thousands of ants beginning to descend on the island. "See the Brooklyn Bridge over there?" he pointed and Adira turned her head. "A whisper that the bridge might collapse caused twelve people to be killed in a stampede." Adira's skin prickled with discomfort at his words.

"Look at all those people who take someone else's idea of heaven and live their lives according to a fantasy. People are so malleable that they believe that God is talking through humans. There is no God." He loosened his grip and turned to her. "I can't believe in a God that would take my child...our child."

"I have to believe," she replied before he could exhale. "I can be angry. I can even hate Him. I have to believe in Him for Tommy. Otherwise, the eight years that he suffered were for nothing." She shook her head in stubborn defiance.

Adrian didn't speak much after that. He just pulled her from place to place. They interacted as if in parallel worlds.

She might as well not have been there at all.

CHAPTER FIFTY-ONE

Elpis remained at the control center. Lately, he couldn't tell whether that was a relief or a burden. After years of being at the heart of it, he was no longer part of the fray. Eleanora had seen to that. Now he had sent those he cared deeply about into it, and every time they left, he had to come to terms with the reality that their sacrifice was part of the job. Although he believed what came next was worth it, he couldn't be sure. He fought with the thought that his decisions might bring them to harm.

"Elpis? Elpis? E? Did you hear me?" Andreas's voice summoned him from his reverie.

"Sorry, what did you ask?" Elpis had a split image on his screen of Clara and Andreas on the south end of Times Square. And Tom and Banko on the north end. There were a few other Go'El dispersed throughout the city.

Clara had insisted on going on the mission rather than staying back at the control center. He hadn't argued with her, although he'd wanted to. Elpis wasn't sure if she was volunteering because of her belief in the mission or her love for Andreas. Memories or not, there was love there that couldn't be shaken. He could see it on both of their faces. Even now, they held hands as they worked their way through the crowd.

"I said, do you see anything on the satellite view? It is too crowded here to use a tablet inconspicuously. Everyone is looking over each other's shoulders. There is tension pulsing through the square. Body temperatures are rising and people who aren't demonstrating are curious, but everyone is paranoid that something is going to happen. Clara's having a hard time distinguishing various light signatures. I have never seen it like this." Andreas's eyes darted from person to person.

Even with her extra sensory gifts, there was too much information for Clara to see everything. She felt her eyes tearing in response to overstimulation.

"I am not seeing much from here. Believe me, I'll let you know. If we don't see something today, my bet will be on the last day. The events will draw an even larger crowd," Elpis reminded them.

Elpis's mind flashed to his blonde counterpart. He wondered if she sat at a desk like his, directing her Poneros followers, reflecting on him and their once unbreakable bond. He wondered if Eleanora ever regretted the missions they had gone on together, fighting for the same cause, holding hands through the battle. He wondered.

Andreas often questioned how Elpis had managed this long without connecting with someone more deeply. He had friends, sure. They had been great friends for a long time, but often Andreas found himself talking about his human life and his memories, while Elpis gave little away. But that didn't stop Andreas from wondering and caring deeply for the happiness of his friend. He protected his memories, Andreas had thought, in a way that kept them sacred. Or perhaps like Pandora's box.

The two men had once had a conversation about the meaning behind their names. Ironically, or he guessed not so ironically, Andreas mean Warrior in Greek. His parents had chosen it because they had come from a time of struggle and war in a country that had preserved its history. It seemed fitting.

Elpis was such an unusual name that no Go'El had ever questioned it, at least not in Andreas's presence. But Andreas decided to question it one day many years ago.

"What does your name mean?" Andreas had asked outright.

Elpis had smiled and leaned back in his chair. They were in a coffee shop in Pakistan after a mission. They had decided to take some time after a rough forty-eight hours before returning to the control center. That kind of relaxation was encouraged amongst the Go'El. It was easy to become disillusioned after the jobs they performed.

"Expectant Hope...like yours, it's Greek." He paused for a moment, deciding if that was enough, but then continued. "Have you ever heard the story of Pandora?" he asked Andreas.

"Sure, hand in the cookie jar concept. Don't do it. Don't open it. It's human nature to find out more about the unknown...and fear it, I guess." Andreas rattled off his memories of lessons in mythology.

"More or less, yes. Pandora was the first woman on Earth. According to Greek myths, Zeus ordered her creation, endowing her with all gifts of beauty, clothing and speech. Along with this, she was given curiosity. So, when she was presented with a box and told not to open it, Zeus knew that she wouldn't be able to stop herself. So she released all of the evils of the world, spreading them over the earth. Quickly, she tried to close the container, but it was too late. Every evil had escaped, but one thing lay at the bottom. The Spirit of Hope, named Elpis." Elpis looked up as he spoke his last sentence, meeting the eyes of his friend. "It is still debated today, whether I made it out of the box." His smile did not reach his eyes; not on that day, at least, and Andreas could not help but wonder about the truth that lay beyond those myths.

CHAPTER FIFTY-TWO

"This is crazy. I keep feeling like I am going to look around and come face to face with my family," Banko kept her head down in a gnawing fear that this could happen.

"Banko, they don't even live in the U.S. I think you're good. Just keep your eyes up and look for a target. I feel like we are flying blind here. This is impossible." Tom's ears were bombarded with scripture from every religious publication.

So far, people had kept to their factions, only responding verbally to their own leaders. However, it was the surrounding crowd that was worrisome. A perimeter of police stood guard with firearms, shields and gasmasks at the ready. Onlookers walked from Christian groups to Muslim groups, to Buddhists and Atheists, moving as if they were looking to purchase secondhand jewelry at an outdoor market.

"Clara told me that on a normal day, one and a half million people pass through Times Square. More than a quarter million work here daily. It's a Friday, so there are at least that many, plus all of these demonstrators. I bet there are close to two million here."

"It has to be a bomb or some sort of chemical weapon," Clara spoke into their ears and he tried not to touch the transmitter in response to the voice. "They wouldn't waste their time on guns, although they may still have them. I am betting they are going to sneak something in here to cause massive damage. I am trying to focus on the light refractions off people. It is most likely a suicide mission and they probably have it strapped to them. Look for large baggy clothing."

Banko and Tom nodded at each other in response and split looks right and then left. He could feel her clench with every possible target. It was still early spring and a cool day. Most people were wearing raincoats.

This wasn't going to be easy.

Then Tom saw a figure standing about twenty meters ahead of them. He tapped Banko and gestured subtly, crossing his hands and running them down his torso in an action indicating he had seen straps. Banko looked at the target and could see the outline of straps through a loosely hung tan jacket. They couldn't tell gender from the back since he or she had a hat covering the outline of the hair that would help in identification. And these days, gender didn't really matter. They both gestured to one another at the same time.

"Clara," Tom touched his earpiece, but spoke softly, "I need your eyes on this target. Can you see anything?"

"I see some sort of faint heat signature radiating off the front of the target, but..." her voice faded as the younger pair approached.

Banko pointed to the target and raised a single finger, then pointed back to Tom. She wanted him to approach first since he would be converging from the front. He would be able to better gauge whether or not the target was holding a detonator or other weapons. The heat signature remained steady, and Tom was now three people away, but the target kept shifting as if he or she anticipated their approach. He looked down to see an alternation shifting from one foot to the other. Tom thought it could be an indicator that the target was about to run. He wrapped his finger tightly around the stunner and slowly popped the snap that kept it in its holster.

As they approached, he felt a nudge from behind that normally wouldn't have caught him off guard. His chest bounced off the woman directly in front of him and he could see the heat signature of an infant asleep inside a sling. "Sorry," he choked out, and kept moving forward.

Banko caught up with him quickly. He smiled at her as he bent over to catch the breath he hadn't realized he'd been holding.

"That was close. Banko, I..." His pleading eyes bore into Banko's.

"Tom, calm down." She placed her warm palm on the back of his neck.

"I'm not sure I can do this. Maybe I was the wrong person to choose." Voicing his fears didn't surprise Banko as much as he thought it might. Her face registered his insecurities without judgment.

"Tom, I have every faith in you to do what's right. You have to fight your own fears. 'On life's journey faith is nourishment, virtuous deeds are shelter, wisdom is the light by day, and right mindfulness is the protection by night. If a man lives a pure life, nothing can destroy him; if he has conquered greed nothing can limit his freedom.'" She stood smiling at him, as if her words were the affirmation that he needed.

Tom stared back at this woman who had been with him since the beginning of his very short new life. She had given him what he needed and asked for nothing in return. She had lent him her faith when he so desperately clung to his fears. "Buddha?" he asked.

"Absolutely," she responded.

"Thank you," Tom whispered squeezing her hand. "Thank you."

They both waited as Elpis spoke. "I could see it, too.

Stick with it. This isn't going to be easy."

Tom took Banko's arm and pulled her to the perimeter of the crowd. They needed a higher elevation. Maybe if they could get out of the crowd, they might notice something they weren't seeing amidst the ocean of people. They saw some commotion just as Tom pulled Banko onto a small cement divider. Unmoving, they watched as patrolmen descended on some teenage boys who had picked up stones from the streets and were hurling them into a Muslim group of demonstrators. Some took a defensive stance as the police cuffed the young men and led them to a squad car.

It was close to that car, near a corner alley, that he saw her.

It was his mother—he knew it had to be her. He knew. Before she disappeared around a corner, he saw a man yanking her arm, pulling her away from the crowd.

He needed to make sure she was all right.

"What is it? What did you see?" Banko whispered, her eyes scanning the masses.

"I saw a woman...my mother. I think it was my mother. I have to make sure she is okay." Tom had already stepped down and was pushing his way through the crowd.

"I'm coming with you," she yelled after him, but she was already too many steps behind to be heard.

CHAPTER FIFTY-THREE

Clara looked down at their tightly entwined fingers and followed her gaze up to the man holding her hand. She felt a comfort she had never known until she had met this man. But she couldn't allow herself this luxury. Trying to focus on the job at hand, she continued scanning. Finally, she said, "Andreas, I was thinking about your story the other day, and about the location of the Go'El. You made a point that we are positioned in places that feel pure; heavenly. Wouldn't the contrast be the dense underpinnings of a city? What if the Poneros are located beneath us here, in a place where humans feel unease and insecurity? Is it possible that those 'Do Not Enter' signs in the length of the subway tunnels may be a doorway to their headquarters?"

Andreas nodded at her logic, but just as he was about to respond, they heard a small voice below them.

"Γιαγιά? Γιαγιά Clara? Is that you?" Clara could do nothing but stare at the little cherub that was calling her by name. "Mommy said you were in heaven. She didn't say...You look weird." The little boy stopped talking and looked at Andreas.

He knows me, Clara thought. Her mouth dropped open and her eyes squinted, forcing some sort of recognition from her hazy human life. It was then that she heard Andreas speak.

"Andreas...I mean Dre. Hello." Andreas extended his hand to the little boy at his waist and bent down, pulling Clara with him. Clara looked from both big Andreas to little, trying to understand the interaction. Then it began to click into place.

"Παππού? Are you Παππού Andreas? I never got to meet you and I really wanted to meet you. Mommy was always saying how wonderful and brave you were and that she wished that I could meet you, but you had to go to heaven too soon. Are you guys on your honeymoon again? Mommy and Daddy are over there. You have to see them." Little Andreas tried to pull his grandparents in the other direction, but his grandfather stopped him gently and knelt down to look into the little boy's face.

"Dre, I feel so lucky to be able to see you, but for now, I really can't see your mommy. We can't stay here. Neither should you. I can see your parents coming and they are very worried about you. Stay right here, don't move. And don't walk away from them in this crowd anymore. They will be here in a minute. Dre, we love you very much. Always remember that. And know...we will see you again." Clara felt the tug on her arm as Andreas pulled her from the little boy.

" Παππούς! Παππούς!" he yelled after them as they moved away. Clara turned back first and heard his words. "Γιαγιά, I saw a car over on the other side by the big TV screen and it was starting to smoke underneath." She smiled at the adorable boy she knew to be her great-grandson and nodded. It was all she could do.

As a new crowd forced themselves between the words that were sent from boy to grandparents, she whipped her head around to face her husband.

"Andreas," she whispered.

CHAPTER FIFTY-FOUR

"*T*om, wait!" Banko no longer worried about who would hear or see her. She knew her friend needed her, no matter what happened next. But as she turned the corner and entered a small alley, she froze.

There stood Tom, his hands braced at his sides. Banko's eyes followed his and she saw the two figures in front of him. There was a woman, about the age she'd guessed Tom's mother to be, but she hadn't yet confirmed that it was her. None of this concerned her when she saw the knife held firmly against the woman's throat.

The man holding it was a slightly older version of Tom.

"Mom, are you okay?" Tom could barely get out the words.

He hadn't really believed it was his mother. The sight of the woman had made him feel nostalgic, and he simply wanted to be sure that the doppelganger was all right. That was what he told himself, until he saw her face.

"I was right." The man pulled the knife smoothly to her neck as if he'd known Tom was behind him. His smirk was sinister, but the rest of his face was familiar. Tom hadn't seen him in years and remembered him only through the haze of childhood. He'd found a picture once that his mother had kept tucked among her minimal belongings long after they'd left him.

He hadn't realized how much his Go'El-self resembled his father.

"I told them it was you. They didn't believe my theory. They patronized me for my own insecurities. I showed them the pictures of you. They were grainy, but they looked too much like me. Except for the eyes. Those are your mother's." He pulled the knife more tightly to her skin, almost as if he had forgotten she was there and only now remembered.

Tom ignored his comments and looked directly at his mother. "How—" She couldn't finish. Adira was speechless.

"Mom, it's me," he let those words hang between them, not having any idea how to convince her.

"What is it you call yourselves? Go'El...rescuer or redeemer in Hebrew, kind of self-proclaiming, don't you think? And how is it that you refer to us? Poneros. Simple. Evil. Good vs. Evil. Doesn't it always come down to that? The difference is that being on the 'right side' is simply a matter of perspective, don't you think? Do you really believe that what we do is wrong? Just as you proclaim yourselves to be redeemers, we are allowing humans to find salvation. Even their Bible references the concept of wiping the slate clean and starting over. People have failed. They have turned on each other, and now they will simply destroy themselves."

Tom began to pace, doing a sort of dance with his father as they both took defensive stances. Banko remained motionless, her mind racing to deduce the best move to release Tom's mother. Beyond the four was a small walkway only wide enough for a single line of people to step through, but also large enough for Adrian to escape, if necessary.

Seeing Tom's eyes move to the opening behind him,

Adrian responded in kind, "You see? You see how people treat one another. That isn't even our doing. It is simply human nature." Adrian slid the knife ever so smoothly across Adira's neck as a crimson line of droplets appeared. Just as Tom made a move to spring, Banko caught his arm.

Adrian laughed as Adira fought for her next breath. "It was so easy. She followed me like a puppy. And you are here, but you can't stop us. We are doing these people a favor. And you can do nothing to stop it." Just as he said it, a riotous sound rose above his voice. He turned Adira slightly to see. Stones were flung from every direction as the Muslim group began to pray in the square. Whether they were being thrown by other religious groups or by bystanders, it wasn't clear, but the police were unable to control the onslaught.

Tom was so defeated by the sight that he didn't take advantage of Adrian's lapse of attention to Adira. She did not move, but searched the face of this young man for some sign that he was the eight-year-old boy she'd so recently buried.

Tom's attention moved back to his mother; he had always been able to give her what she needed.

"Do you see, Son, how with the freedom of choice, humans will choose what is easy rather than what is right. They've had their chance, and they have failed. Now it is our turn." His grip on Adira tightened, pulling her arms together more tightly behind her back and forcing the knife inflexibly against her jugular.

"You are no father of mine, and you are wrong, because I have something that you don't, and it will make good prevail every time." Tom pulled his left heel onto the interior of his right.

Adrian again tightened his grip on the knife and altered his footing only slightly.

"People are inherently good. Sometimes they just need a little push." He tipped his chin toward the crowd behind them. The stones had ceased to fly and a circle had formed around the praying Muslims. Christians, Jews, Atheists, Buddhists, Hindus and dozens of onlookers had created an unbreakable chain around the vulnerable group. They had created a human wall to protect those devout in their beliefs. And in turn the police had contained the rabble-rousers who had instigated tragedy.

Adrian's head had turned in disbelief, and Banko and Tom took advantage. Tom clicked the release on his boot holster springing a knife into his hands. But before they could enact their plan, Adira surprised them both by slamming her heel onto the top of Adrian's foot. She followed it up with a snapping blow to his chin with her right elbow.

Adira was drenched in blood. But, it was not her own.

CHAPTER FIFTY-FIVE

"*H*ow could you lie?" Clara exploded. "You said relationships couldn't be based on lies. You said that to me, just days ago! You should have stayed away. You should have left me alone. I had a job to do. You knew you were distracting me." Her words split Andreas apart.

"I couldn't stay away," was all he could say. His voice was weak.

"Now what? I'm supposed to pretend it isn't tearing me apart that I can't remember the moments that make people human. I'm not real, Andreas. I don't exist. How can you be with someone who doesn't exist?" Clara couldn't stop moving. Her gesticulations were growing wild. Even as she spoke, she was aware that her emotions were being made public through their coms, but she was past the point of caring.

Andreas tried to reach for her, but she pulled back. He returned his hand to his side, awkwardly. As if it didn't belong there.

"I'm not me anymore." Her eyes lifted to this 'husband' who'd had a lifetime of her inside his mind, and she wondered if it was resentment of that which was paralyzing her. "I think Elpis is wrong. I can't stop this. Look around us." She gestured to the commotion around the open prayer. "People don't want us. Even if they knew, they don't want our help. And I don't think I have what it takes to change that."

The silence amongst the Go'El was deafening. It drowned out the yelling emanating from the humans behind them. Andreas opened his hands in supplication and dropped to his knees in front of her. He did not dare touch her, but his mind searched for the words that could bring his Clara back to him. His mind flipped through the rolodex of reminiscence that was their human life together. He had waited all these years enveloped in the faith that when the time was right, he would have her again. He never lost focus on that, even through the long years of despondency that could be the life of a Go'El.

He looked into eyes that reflected a soul that was all Clara's, even if she didn't remember it. "Clara, even if you have no recollection of your former self, I do. And I will fill your mind with every nuance of that person, if that's what you want."

"How can you trust a person with no humanity?" Clara's eyes begged him to answer.

"Just as it was before, it is again. Together, we are stronger."

"I knew it," Clara offered softly.

"Clara..."

She stopped him before he could begin. "I understand why you couldn't tell me. And I'm not sure I would have believed you. At least not at first... But I knew. I think there was some part of me that wanted to be the woman you spoke of. Your wife," she tasted the title on her lips and paused. "I wanted you to give me back the memories that I had lost. I wanted it to be you. I'm so sorry."

"Sorry for what? You seem to think that because you have lost your past, you are not my Clara. But your soul is the same. No transformation can take that from you. You treat people with kindness; you see and feel everything around you and take on others' pain. You exist in a place where real living begins. Why are you apologizing?" He smiled then, his sky-blue eyes sparkling.

"That might not be enough." She leaned out of Andreas's embrace and looked at the crowd still locked in adversity.

Elpis spoke now. "Clara, you have left me with avenues to take that may just be the absolution we need." A tear freed itself from Clara's eyes and Andreas took the opportunity to wipe it away. "Even if you don't feel it, Clara, you have already done your job. It is one that never ends, but you have saved so many in such a short time. It isn't selfishness to want more from your existence; it is a destination."

It was Andreas's turn to comfort. His finger turned her face toward him. "I will remember for you."

She laughed and pressed her lips to his. She ran her fingers through the short dark curls on the back of his neck that begged for her touch. A picture, she was guessing, that may have been repeated from their honeymoon. "I love you."

"I have always loved you." Andreas dipped his forehead to hers.

As they rose together, their eyes fell on the scene around them. Rows upon rows of Athoos protecting people they didn't know, people who believed in different gods and different myths. None of that mattered; this was the picture of humanity.

CHAPTER FIFTY-SIX

They arrived at the car just as Tom and Banko approached with another woman. Elpis positioned his players as he saw fit, and kept each apprised of the other's progress. Banko began the inspection, just as she had been trained.

It didn't take long for her to find the source of the smoke.

Those that had been trained knew instantly not to open doors, start the engine or affect the accelerator for fear that it would detonate a bomb. Andreas dipped beneath the drivetrain and quickly came back out.

"We have one minute," he said calmly. Clara nodded in response. Their minds worked in tandem. A solution had already surfaced.

"I'll do it," Tom volunteered. Banko stepped forward with him.

"There isn't any time," Clara responded touching a finger to her ear. She looked at Andreas as she removed her Ankh to open the portal.

"Together," he said.

"Together," she repeated.

There was no doubt.

"Tom, this is your time. I've had mine, and every moment has been worth it. Now it's my time to be with Clara." Looking back, he smiled at the wife he had been waiting so long to hold. He reached out to shake Tom's hand.

Adira now pulled her son closer as Andreas said a last goodbye to Banko. "Take care of him," he gestured to Tom. "You are an impeccable fighter and an even better friend. I'm glad he has you." With that, he turned back to Clara.

"Andreas, how do you know that you'll be together after this?" Tom gestured to the car and to the husband and wife of which he'd grown so fond.

Andreas turned back and pulled Clara snuggly to his side, looking at her as if no one else existed. "Because I have faith..."

Andreas and Clara placed their hand solidly on the explosive before them. Andreas gave her one last smile. She smiled back. To Elpis, he said, "It's been an honor, my friend."

They both closed their eyes as a blinding light sent them hurtling beyond, the unsuspecting Athoos remaining safely behind.

EPILOGUE

**"But the Hebrew word, the word timshel—
'Thou mayest'—that gives a choice. It might
be the most important word in the world.
That says that way is open. That throws it
right back on the man. For if 'Thou mayest'—
it is also try that 'Thou mayest not."** —
John Steinbeck, *East of Eden*

*"I*t isn't over." His weakness for the lines in her face, framed by the blonde sensation of the sun overwhelmed him. Elpis had lost much today, but he had also gained. She spoke to him as if he hadn't known the outcome.

"And it may never be," he returned. The fatigue of his last days was washing over him, but he had to see her. He knew that things would be changing.

"You know what He'll do." Eleanora's shaking voice betrayed her desperation. "It has to escalate. A human knows of your existence."

"Just remember, Eleanora. Remember the Third Reich,

remember the Crusades. We faced it before and we will do it again." Elpis's resolve straightened his spine as he fought to move away from her.

Once again, he turned before she did, out of self-preservation, he thought. But he heard her soft whisper carry over the wind.

"Why do you stay?" she questioned.

He stopped, but did not turn. "You know why."

ACKNOWLEDGMENTS

David and Kelly at Open Books—Thank you for seeing something in my "weird connections" that made RFM worth publishing.

I am indebted to my big fat Greek family, especially Mom, Dad, Kent, and Cathy, for all that you do to create more memories for us all. Also, to my newest family who accepts me as a daughter and sister. Without you, Marianne, Lee, Liz and Pete, (and Summer) my family would not be complete. (Liz—thank you especially, for reading the random texts I sent, editing and encouraging! It's your turn!) Stephanie, Steve, Nick, Alex, Kristin and Allison—Your excitement made this feel real. Stephanie, thank you for always editing and listening when I need you.

The DBC—Thank you for teaching me to laugh and love life always! Especially to Joanie for believing in me from the start. Without you, this book would never have become such. Kate, thank you for making me believe this was worth pursuing and editing whenever I needed you. Gus, Dribin, and Ellen—I needed you and you dropped everything to read for me! Thank you! Angela and Carrie, you are amazing at editing my words and my sanity.

My current and former students near and far- look for some of your names and ideas in here...you have taught me so much!

Logan and Cora—Without you, our lives would feel soulless. You made me realize what all this was about. Don't ever be afraid to fail!

Gavin—You give me wings and armor that make me feel like I can do anything.

ABOUT THE AUTHOR

Diana Tarant Schmidt loves getting lost in a story, and it is that love that is the undercurrent to all that she does.

For fourteen years she has taught junior high school, and she shares her love of stories with her students.

Through teaching, Diana has also gained an enthusiasm for service. With the help of her students, she executes several projects each year, donating money, objects and time to various organizations in the Chicago area where she lives and works.

When not teaching, she and her husband find time for small adventures. Diana's favorites include playing sports, mountain hiking and travel.

Outside the classroom, Diana writes curriculum and raises two incredible humans along with the best partner and true superhero imaginable.

Made in the USA
Lexington, KY
26 October 2016